"Thanks for all your help." *Not.* Other than standing there, he hadn't done a thing to help with Horace.

He held a hand out to her. "Looked like you had him under control."

Darcy rose onto her elbows. *Yuck.* Her jeans were caked with mud and who knew what else. Anxious to get out of the stench, she placed her hand in his. Palm to palm, her heart skipped a beat, and she forgot to breath.

He tugged on her arm, pulling her to her feet. His arm went around her waist as she slammed into his chest. The unexpected heat of him made her step back into one of Horace's holes, knocking them both off balance.

Nick twisted, bracing her against his hard chest as they landed back in the muck. Air whooshed from her lips. She stared at his mud-splattered form in horror.

Oh, God, he's sure to fire me now.

"I'm so sorry. Are you okay?" She tugged her foot to free it, catching her boot on the cuff of his jeans.

"I would be if you'd stop kicking me." All movement halted on her part as she stared, biting her bottom rim to keep from laughing as she wiped the specks of mud from his cheek, making the damage ten times worse. His skin was warm and bristly under her finger, and she quickly withdrew her hand.

His chest rumbled beneath her.

Startled by the warmth that spread through her, she levitated herself by placing her palms on his chest.

"You should see yourself." His lips lifted at the corners before he broke out in a full laugh.

Lost Memories

by

Sherri Thomas

Honky Tonk Hearts

This is a work of fiction. Names, characters, places, and incidents are either the product of the author's imagination or are used fictitiously, and any resemblance to actual persons living or dead, business establishments, events, or locales, is entirely coincidental.

Lost Memories

COPYRIGHT © 2013 by Sherri Thomas

Cover Art by *Tamra Westberry*

The Wild Rose Press, Inc.
PO Box 708
Adams Basin, NY 14410-0708
Visit us at www.thewildrosepress.com

Publishing History
First Yellow Rose Edition, 2013
Digital ISBN 978-1-61217-743-4
Print ISBN 978-1-62830-154-0

Honky Tonk Hearts
Published in the United States of America

Dedication

This is for my husband.
I couldn't ask for a better best friend.
Thank you for all the wonderful memories
and many more to come.

Prologue

"Good morning, Darcy." Dr. Sheffield entered the room with a smile on his lips. He crossed to the foot of the bed and picked up the chart. "How are you feeling?"

Darcy Brooks gave a short laugh. "You mean besides the fact the only reason I even know my name is because it's on the driver's license found in my purse?" Bitterness lined her tone, but she didn't care.

"I see anger has set in."

She slapped the mattress and glanced at the back of her cut up hands. The puckered, red marks sparked her temper even more. "It's damn frustrating." Waking up in a strange Texas hospital over a week ago wasn't her idea of luck.

"I know this has been quite an ordeal for you, but you're doing wonderful." He flipped through the chart. "Any memories surfacing?" Hazel eyes narrowed beneath bushy gray brows as he moved to her side.

"A few, but they're fuzzy," she lied. Her memory wasn't any closer to returning today than the day the eighteen-wheeler smashed into her car. One major bump on the head and bang—everything had vanished. Her mind a clean slate. Ten whole days later and she still remembered *nothing*.

"Don't rush it." The doctor patted her shoulder.

"These things take time."

Time, ha. She spent too many hours in this infirmary, and with not one visitor other than hospital staff to check on her injuries.

Dr. Sheffield hooked the file back on the foot of the bed before returning to extract a small penlight out of his white lab coat pocket. He ran the beam past her pupils. "The good news is other than a few minor cuts and bruises, your physical health is good and your vitals are stable. Even your CAT scan and MRI came back normal." He straightened and put his penlight away, then folded his hands in front of his flat stomach. "However, I am concerned about letting you go home."

"Why?" Darcy frowned and shook her head; the motion set off a headache. She clasped her hands tight in her lap to keep from rubbing the pain away and winced as the sores on her tender skin stung under the pressure. Small cuts from the glass of the windshield also marred her arms, neck, and face. Her leg sported the worst of the markings with an angry, red, seven-inch slash running horizontally across the inside of her left thigh.

"I don't like the idea of you going home to an empty house. I think it'd be best to move you to the rehabilitation building for a couple of weeks."

No! Desperation clawed at her throat and white walls glared in her sights as her vision swam. The pull on her heart, the desire to find out the details of her life proved too hard to ignore. If she didn't find another soul to shed light on her existence, she'd be at the mercy of strangers forever. On the other hand, if she talked the doctors into letting her leave, what waited for her outside the sterile walls? She hadn't the slightest idea of where she came from. No recollection of family—*if* one existed. Did she have a husband? Children? A mother or father?

For heaven's sake, it's not as if I dropped out of the sky.

"I think I'd be fine." Squaring her shoulders and raising her chin, she hoped her voice didn't reveal the fear.

"I'm sorry." He shook his balding head. "I'm not comfortable with you being alone. At least not for the time being."

She put her head back on the pillow and shut her eyes. Any sliver of optimism she held teetered close to the edge.

"It's our only option at this point. Unless someone comes forward within the next twenty-four hours, we're going to need to move you."

He pulled the bandage off her forehead with a quick tug. She sucked in a deep breath to ward off the sting of the tape.

The doctor inspected the wound at her hairline. "Now, have you talked with social services regarding your medical bills? They can help you apply for assistance."

"Yes, but without knowing my background, it's going to take a lot of work. For now I've agreed to make payments once I find a job." The world moved at a turbulent speed, running over anyone who paused in the process.

"I don't want you going out to find employment the day you're discharged. Nevertheless, it is good to get your ducks in a row." He patted her shoulder again. "You rest now. I'll send the nurse in to change the bandage on your leg and head." The door clicked behind him, leaving her alone to the deafening silence.

Darcy threw the white covers back. Her raw body protested as she forced her legs across the floor to the window. She needed something to jog her memory before she went stark raving mad. When she first woke up, she'd been terrified, and later, when the nurse showed her the purse, she tore through it trying to find something, *anything*. But the bag contained nothing but makeup and her picture on a driver's license.

A *new* driver's license.

No credit cards. No pictures. No letters. Nada. According to the landlord of the apartment listed on her license, she'd moved to Amarillo, Texas, only a few weeks ago. And as far as he knew, she had yet to move her belongings here.

Then he asked if she'd be retaining the apartment for future use or if she'd be terminating her lease—not one word of concern for her well-being.

She rested the unmarked side of her forehead on the warm glass of the window. The sun shone high in the afternoon sky, and she squinted at the people coming in and out of the doors below. That's what she wanted, to be free to come and go as she pleased.

Why did I move to Texas? Did she have relatives in the area, a friend?

Darcy crossed back to her bed, her body trembling with the effort. Why did this happen to her? Was she a bad person and the Big Guy upstairs wanted to punish her? She sat back and closed her eyes. Nothing. And the hardest part was being at the mercy of strangers.

"Hi, Darcy," a female voice said from the door. "You awake?"

"Yeah." She opened her eyes and pushed herself up further on the bed before giving Jordan Reece a grim smile.

"You certainly don't look happy." The blonde nurse placed the materials she held in her hands on the bedside table.

"Just another day of not remembering who the hell I am," she blurted out, then bit her lip.

Guilt ate at her for snapping. Over the past week and a half, the RN had become her friend, the one person she confided in. The nurturing woman had listened to Darcy rant and rave over her situation and showed nothing but compassion. She'd even taken time to stop by for nightly card games and shared her own problems with an ex-boyfriend.

"I'm sorry. I don't mean to take this out on you."

"Aw, hon. I'm sure it'll come back to you."

A glove-covered hand smoothed the hair back from her forehead.

"On the upside, this is healing nicely. I don't think the scar will be too noticeable."

Cold, medicated cream and a bandage applied to the area made her shudder.

"Now, let's have a look at your leg."

Darcy scooted down on the bed and moved the blankets out of the way.

"I see the night nurse applied more tape." Jordan placed a hand on her thigh and pulled the first piece quick.

Hissing through her teeth at the sudden pain, Darcy glanced down to see if the adhesive ripped off her skin.

"I'm sorry. I know that hurt." The caregiver pulled another strip. "That's it. Take a deep breath. Almost done. One more to go."

Stomach churning, she inhaled through her nose. She placed a hand across her belly in hopes of fighting off the nausea as the smells of disinfectants in the air contributed to her queasiness.

"There, all done." The sterile dressing landed in the garbage pail. "Not too bad. Dr. Sheffield might remove the sutures in a day or two."

Darcy stared at the stitches holding the gash on her leg together and grimaced. The dark pieces of thread were a sharp contrast to the pale, sensitive skin. According to the good doctor, a large piece of glass from the windshield had embedded itself into her skin, missing her femoral artery by mere inches.

Jordan poured a cup of water from the pitcher on the stand and held it out. "Here drink this."

Taking the cup in her scabbed hand, she sipped the liquid, quenching her parched throat.

"Better?"

"Yes, thanks."

"You bet." The nurse placed the cup back on the table and applied a new dressing over the stitches, then drew the sheet over Darcy's legs. "Now, why don't you tell me what has you in such a rotten mood."

"Don't you have other patients to tend?"

"I have a few minutes." Her friend pulled the chair closer and sat down. "Spill it."

She sighed. "Dr. Sheffield isn't comfortable sending me home alone. He wants to move me to the rehab unit."

"Is that all?" The blue-eyed woman waved her hand through the air. "Geeze, rehab isn't that bad."

Jordan remained the one person Darcy figured

might have understood. *Guess not.*

"I feel like I'm in a time warp. I want to go home, to get on with my life." She gave a short spurt of laughter. "Whatever that may hold."

"I know, but you have to do what the doctor says. He's only looking to your best interest."

"I'm serious." She balled the sheets in her palm and bit back the tears as pain ripped through her fist. "I'll go insane if I have to stay confined in this hospital much longer."

"You're in luck, then. The mental ward has a few empty beds." She grinned wide.

Darcy glared and exhaled through her nose.

"Sorry. Bad joke." Jordan got up, smoothed the front of her burgundy uniform and crossed to the window. "Hmm. I wonder."

"What?"

"I'm thinking, give me a minute." Her friend paced back and forth, tapping a finger to her lips before whipping back around. "You know, I've been looking for a roommate for the past month without any luck. Would you be interested in moving in with me for a while? I think Dr. Sheffield will agree, since you won't be alone...and I am a nurse."

Darcy's spirits lifted, then plummeted. "What about rent? He doesn't want me working yet."

"I'm not worried about the money. I can afford the place myself. I only want a roommate because it's too much house for one person, and I hate living alone."

"I can't freeload off you."

"Nonsense." A dismissive hand waved through the air.

"I mean it." Flinging the sheets aside, she swung

her legs to the side of the bed. "When I'm released for work, I'll pay you back rent from the day I move in."

"We'll work it out later. For now, I'll talk to Dr. Sheffield before he leaves for the day."

"Thank you so much for this." Not caring about her physical state, she bounced off the bed and wrapped her arms tight around her friend.

"Hey, you're doing me a favor too. Now I won't have to come home to an empty house." She chuckled, returning the embrace before leaving the room.

As the door shut, Darcy smiled. For the first time since she woke up ten days ago, the sun shone bright both outside and in.

Chapter One

A mass of nerves knotted in Darcy's belly. This was what she wanted, right? A job? Independence? To live again?

She continued driving down the road and turned the radio up. Country-western blared from the car speakers, easing her anxiety. Music, she'd learned over the past six months, helped to clear her head and soothe her jangled nerves. Singing to the latest hit, she turned into the driveway of the Matthews Dude Ranch, then hit the brakes. The song died on her lips.

Flicking the radio off, she stared out the windshield in awe of the massive wooden structure. Tammy Matthews hadn't described her home as being quite this luxurious. Windows upon windows lined the first floor extending close to the roof on the far end of the inn. The three-story log bed and breakfast resembled one of those vacationing ski lodges she saw in magazines.

Pulling to the side where gravel filled a parking area, she cut the engine. Her uneasiness grew as she reached for the hair clip in the console and corralled her wayward strands back from her face.

"Please, don't let me screw this up," she prayed, then breathed deep as four cowboys came out to the wrap-around porch. Tammy had told her not to let her sons intimidate her, but even at this distance, the four were of impressive size.

"Oh, God."

Darcy stepped out on shaky legs as one of the men descended the stairs and continued toward her.

"Afternoon, ma'am." He touched the brim of his Stetson. "Can I help you with something?" He smiled, flashing perfect white teeth as dark eyes raked over her.

A dog barked and ambled over, nuzzling her hand with a wet nose. She bent down to pat the golden-colored canine. A big, wet tongue tickled her skin making her laugh as the dog wagged its tail.

"Dakota, enough." He moved the dog away with a hand on his scruff. "Sorry, he has no manners."

"That's okay. I love dogs."

She glanced at the cowboy from beneath lowered lashes. His deep voice vibrated through her when he spoke while his gaze warmed her skin from the top of her head to the toes of her boots. Darcy pulled herself to her full five feet two inch height, but only came to the cowboy's chest.

Eyes narrowed in her direction. "What can I help you with?"

"I'm looking for Nick Matthews."

"You found him." He frowned. "And you are?"

"Darcy Brooks." She stuck out her hand.

A suspicious expression crossed his features as he reached out, his hand swallowing hers. He squinted. "I'm sorry, I'm at a loss here. Do I know you?"

Oh no, did Tammy not tell them I was arriving today?

She raised her chin determined not to let his scowl daunt her. "Mrs. Matthews, your mom, said today at one o'clock would be a good time to get settled in."

"My mother's out of town. She must have forgotten to write you in the books."

Nick gave a half grin. At least she hoped he smiled, for the action resembled a snarl to her.

"Let's go get you registered."

He spun on his heel, giving her full view of his denim-clad butt. A tighter, nicer ass she'd never seen. She wiped the sweat from her forehead with the back of her hand. Even though the clouds covered the sun's rays, the heat had picked up a few degrees.

Darcy shook her head and sprinted to catch up with his longer strides. When she reached his side, he slowed his pace.

"When will the rest of your group be joining you?" he asked, glancing toward her.

"What group?" She brought her sights to his and lost herself in the chocolate depths. No sounds registered as she stared in a daze...until her foot hit a rock and she stumbled forward.

A massive hand circled her elbow, strong and sure, preventing her from falling on her face. A static charge zapped her skin where his fingers held her.

"You vacationing alone?" A muscle twitched in his cheek as he dropped his hand and placed one boot on the bottom step of the porch. "We normally schedule in groups, but I guess we can make revisions to our normal program."

"Oh, I'm not here for a vacation. Mrs. Matthews hired me to take over for Theresa."

Nick looked her up and down, then gave what sounded to her like a derogatory snort. She took offense to his attitude. From what Tammy told her, Theresa's shoes would not be easily filled. Apparently, the woman had worked with the animals, organized the overnight trips, planned entertainment, and dealt with the female drama of the guests. Not that Tammy expected her to take on every detail right away—at least that's what she'd told her.

"When was this?"

"I met with your mom a few times over the last three weeks actually." Shouldn't he know this? Tammy is *his* mother, and this is his family's ranch? "She officially gave me the job last week." Not liking the way this meeting was starting out, she placed her hands on her hips to let him know she wouldn't back down from her only job prospect.

"Is that so?" Thick arms folded over his wide chest.

"Yes." *Does he seriously think I'm making this up?*

"Funny, she didn't say anything to me."

What am I to do now? In an effort to appear indifferent, she shrugged. "That's a moot point as far as I'm concerned." From the moment Jordan came home and told her of the conversation with a patient's wife regarding a possible job opportunity on a ranch, Darcy wanted the job.

His brows drew together. "Let's go inside and see if we can't find out what's going on."

She followed him up the stairs to where the three other cowboys waited.

"Miss Brooks, these are my brothers, Sam, Trent, and Chris. Guys, Darcy Brooks is apparently here to take over Theresa's job."

She caught the sarcastic edge to his voice, but relaxed as each brother smiled and shook her hand. Dark hair, brown eyes, and similar bone structures linked the four physically. Darcy prayed the resemblance stopped there and each possessed a different mind-set than Nick. If not, she was in for a long ride.

He pulled the screen door open and motioned for her to enter.

As she passed, her arm brushed his chest. Awareness shot through her. Having not been around many men in the past six months, the reaction was only natural. *Yeah, I'll stick with that explanation.*

She clasped her hands together and sucked in much needed air as the hard-nosed cowboy hung his hat by the door. One by one, his brothers followed suit before Nick led the group down the narrow hall to an office.

Sunlight shone through large windows behind a mahogany desk with papers cluttered on one corner. A tan leather couch and a couple of chairs filled the space. The area screamed business and male. The masculine scent in the room wrapped around her.

"Have a seat," Nick instructed as he sat behind the desk.

Darcy lowered herself into the chair closest to the table as the others stood along side of her.

"Since my mother isn't here, and we had no idea you applied for the position, I'd like some information before we go any further." He raised a doubtful brow.

"Okay." She gripped the arms of the chair to quell her shaking hands. *Don't show your fear. Isn't that what they say when you're being stalked by an animal?* Considering that's exactly how she felt, in this instance, she assumed the same rule applied.

"Chris, why don't you see if you can get Mom on the phone while we get started."

"Sure thing," the youngest brother answered, then left the room.

"First off, do you have a résumé or physical from your doctor? Without a physical, I can't allow you to start work."

The man certainly wasted no time with pleasantries.

"I gave the forms to Mrs. Matthews."

Nick grabbed a pile of papers from the corner of the desk and shuffled through the contents before slapping the stack. He pulled open the top drawer then a side drawer before producing a manila folder. Flipping open the file, he scanned the pages, frowned a couple times and shook his head. "You don't list much of a job history."

Darcy cringed. *This is it. He's going to take one look at the light list of experience and tell me to get off the ranch.* Not knowing her own past made for unexplained years of her life and therefore vague information on her résumé.

"I moved here a short time ago," she stated.

After being turned down for job after job before this one, she'd made the decision not to reveal her amnesia to Tammy. She settled a hand on her purse, where the paper from Dr. Sheffield explaining her accident and the extent of her injuries remained tucked safely away.

Nick's brows grew together. "What about before you moved?"

"The company I worked for went out of business. I have no idea how to reach them."

He picked up a pen. "What was the name of the company? Your boss? How about an old address even?"

"Ah..." *Think. Think.*

"Hey, Nick, slow down. Don't browbeat her." Sam moved to his side, winked at Darcy, and picked up the résumé.

"I couldn't reach Mom," Chris said, entering the room. "I left a message for her to call."

"You could've at least offered her something to drink," Sam continued to Nick, then nodded in her direction. "Would you like coffee or water, maybe sweet tea?"

"No, thank you." She smiled at this brother's easygoing nature. Though a smidgen shorter than Nick, he sported a beefier build and kinder face.

"Our ma really did raise us to be gentleman." Chris chuckled. "Nick must have a burr up his shorts."

"Chris, cool it." Nick ran a hand through his dark hair and down the back of his neck before leaning forward on his desk to address Darcy again. "Do you have any references?"

"They're on the back of my résumé." Jordan and Ms. Nancy from the animal shelter were the only people she knew to vouch for her character.

"I'd know that if Sam would give me back the paper," the eldest brother growled, reaching for the sheet.

Chris moved to stand beside the middle brother, who yanked the résumé further away from Nick. "You worked at the animal shelter?"

Finally, a question she was able to answer. "Yes. I volunteered there for the past four months."

"They do good work. I think Sam finds most of his four-legged friends through Ms. Nancy's contacts." A mischievous grin came closer. Eyes danced with laughter as Chris whispered, "They're his only friends by the way."

Darcy found her tight shoulder muscles loosening a bit and smiled.

"Very funny, runt." The stockiest brother chuckled and put an elbow to Chris's ribs.

Darcy watched the exchange between the brothers and felt her lip dip slightly in frustrated sadness. Did she have siblings? A sister? A brother? And if so, had they joked and prodded each other in fun banter as these brothers did? Were they worried about her now?

"Can you guys be serious for ten minutes?" Nick scolded.

"Lighten up." Sam shook his head and rolled his eyes.

"Let's talk about Nick's shortcomings later. I'm sure Miss Brooks has better things to do than sit here listening to us bicker." Trent sighed, impatience evident in his tone.

Darcy turned toward the frustrated sigh. Up until now, she'd forgotten another Matthews sat on the couch behind her.

He gave her a tight-lipped smirk.

"Trent's right. Sorry," Sam said and lowered the paper. "You moved here six months ago?"

"Yes." She faced the three at the desk again.

"Where'd you live before this?"

Wishing for the glass of sweet tea she declined to quench her parched throat, she swallowed. "A small town up north. I don't think it even registers on the map." In an attempt to hide her nervousness, she laughed.

"I'm sure I can find it, *if* you can give me a name."

Nick's dark eyes bore into her. Maybe this job wasn't such a good idea after all.

Be honest and tell him about your amnesia.

Nope. No can do.

The manager at the last job she applied for refused to hire her, claiming the decision had nothing to do with her accident, but she knew different. Everywhere she went people were wary of hiring a person with an existing medical condition, especially because she possessed no past. No work experience. No qualifications.

Darcy wanted this job more than anything. Wanted a sense of self-worth, to be a whole person, and she'd be damned if she'd allow some cowboy to bully her.

She stuck her chin up and straightened in the chair. "It's a little town in northern Pennsylvania called Girard." She fought back a groan at the lie.

"Do you have family around these parts?" The uncompassionate brother questioned.

"No."

"What brought you to Amarillo?"

"My friend, Jordan Reece, lives here. She's a nurse at the hospital. That's how I met your mom."

And that's as close to the truth as she chanced explaining. The questions came too fast, and she didn't have time to think. Her bravado wavered under the pressure, and she shifted in her chair. Her gaze clashed with Nick's and heat crept up her cheeks.

When his eyes narrowed, her insides twisted into a tight knot. The air grew thick, and she licked her dry lips. He followed the movement of her tongue, and her breathing escalated as her heart hammered in her ears.

"Nick." One of the brothers nudged him in the arm. "The phone's ringing."

He swiped up the receiver. "H-hello." He coughed, clearing his throat. "Hey, Mom. Yes, I know. I'm not. We can handle it. That's not nec—" He rolled his eyes upward; the other brothers chuckled, and Nick raised a hand, silencing the trio. "Okay. Okay. I can't talk about it now. Yes, she's right here." He turned Darcy's way. "Mmm-hmm. You could have told us. Fine." He held out the phone, his lips set in a grim line. "My mother."

Her gaze jumped from each man, and then to the receiver stuck out in front of her. Careful not to touch his hand, she pulled the device from him with two fingers.

"She wants to talk to Darcy, and we're to leave the room," Nick informed his brothers as he stood.

When the brothers filed out and shut the door, Darcy raised the phone to her ear.

"H-hello."

"Darcy, how are you? I'm sorry I couldn't be there to welcome you, but I forgot Nick Sr. had scheduled this trip."

"Th—"

"With his near heart attack this past year," Tammy continued, "I want to take advantage of any time we can sneak away together."

"Mrs. Matthews, I—"

"Call me Tammy. I thought we covered that during our luncheons. Calling me Mrs. Matthews makes me sound old. Not that having four grown boys doesn't make me feel old at times, but I'm only in my fifties for Heaven's sake. Okay, let's get down to business."

Darcy chuckled. She couldn't help it. The woman

contained a strong similarity to a tornado swooping in.

"I sent them out because I wanted a chance to reassure you. I know my boys can be a bit overwhelming, which was why I met with you outside the ranch in the first place. I wanted to get to know you as a person before I introduced you. I needed to be sure you could handle the stress of four testosterone-filled cowboys who, frankly, don't always think with the right head, if you know what I mean."

Darcy laughed, picturing Tammy leaning forward, brushing her long, sandy-blonde hair off her shoulder and raising her eyebrows as she had whenever she made one of her wild comments during their lunches. The woman didn't pull any punches.

"I know we covered the basics during our lunches, but now that you've met my boys, what do you think?"

Tammy had quizzed her during the meetings; was she married, did she have family in the area, did she know first aid and CPR. The last two were the only questions answered honestly thanks to Jordan's request that she take classes.

"I...I'm not sure what you mean." She stood and moved toward the window. The barns sat off in the distance with pasture upon rolling pasture surrounding the big buildings.

Hearty laughter in her ear pulled her away from the beautiful landscaping.

"I want your honest opinion on how the world sees my boys. How do they come off to other people? I want to know how they act when I'm not there. I need to make sure they can handle running the place without us there, you see. I realize you just met them, but what's your first impression?"

"Oh. Um..." Weren't her *boys* too old for her to worry about? "Sam seems sweet, but strong. Trent, I'm not real sure. He hangs in the background. Chris is a character." A vision of him poking fun at his brothers filtered in, and she giggled. "He's free spirited, and I think a jokester. But I don't know. I really haven't had much time to talk to them."

"What about Nick? You skipped him, honey," Tammy's voice sounded amused.

She frowned at the receiver in her hand. This conversation struck her as odd to say the least.

"Darcy?"

"Um..." How to explain Nick? *Hot. Mysterious. Judgmental.*

"Are you there?"

"Yes, sorry. Ah...Nick, he's harder than the rest. I mean, he's intense." Her mind played back his powerful eyes, his chiseled features and slightly crooked nose. She sat on the low windowsill behind the desk. "He has an electrical...I mean a take-charge attitude about him." She chewed on her nail. Did she say too much?

"An electrical charge, you say?" A chuckle vibrated through the phone line and Tammy's voice lowered. "You definitely have a take on him...them. It's been a pleasure talking with you. I do apologize again for not being there."

"Thank you for taking a chance on me."

"Thank you, dear. Now, do me a favor and put Nick back on the phone."

"Hold on, I'll find him for you." She crossed to the door and pulled it open to find the hall empty. Taking a deep breath, she walked toward the entrance.

"Nick?" Where did everyone go?

She didn't want to be searching around in the strange surroundings. Moving to the next doorway, she glanced inside the empty room and backed up into the hallway.

Not sure of where to look next, she spun on her heel and stopped dead in her tracks millimeters from a massive chest. Her body tingled with nervous awareness.

Oh, Lord, what have I gotten myself into?

Chapter Two

Nick glanced down at the beautiful woman in front of him. His hand itched to free the soft, dark curls secured in some sort of elastic thing. When she first stepped from her vehicle, he was curious over what such a gorgeous female would be doing way out here. Then as he neared and his heart beat out of his chest, he wondered over asking her out. Too bad she was holding something back, evident by her fidgeting demeanor and facial features. If there was one thing Miss Brooks was not good at, it was lying. Her doe eyes gazed up, and he moved forward a half step.

A flush rose to her cheeks, and she stepped back.

"Tammy...er...your mom wants to speak with you."

A smirked twitched his lip at her uneasiness as he took the phone from her hand.

"Thanks. Chris is out on the porch waiting to show you around."

He watched her denim-covered behind hurry out the door before raising his mother's screeching voice to his ear.

"Nick...Darcy...is anyone there?"

"You have her calling you Tammy?" he asked, returning to the den.

"Seems fitting since she'll be working on the ranch."

"Mom, you can't be serious about hiring her."

"I'm completely serious, Nicholas, and I expect you to treat her kindly."

"What do you know about this woman?"

When his mother informed him of her plan to hire another female to fill Theresa's duties, Nick tried making her see reason. Another cowboy would've worked out a lot better, but his mother was adamant in her thinking. She claimed the female guests were more comfortable with a woman on staff. In the end, as usual, Nick lost the argument, and her view of the situation made his life a living hell.

After his brothers interviewed a couple of women she didn't approve of, claiming "those girls" were only after her boys, not a job, she decided to do the interviewing herself.

Darcy flashed before his eyes. With her brandy-colored hair and big, brown eyes, she'd be a definite distraction. Five feet of trouble.

He rolled his tense shoulders. "Why didn't you tell us about her?"

"I'm sorry, honey. You know how busy I've been trying to keep your father from constantly worrying over the ranch; it must have slipped my mind."

"Mom, you can't hire her. She's hiding something. I know it." Being the oldest made it his job to protect and guide his brothers. A job he'd failed at a while back. One he refused to fail again.

He shook his head. *Another time. Another place.*

"And *how* do you know that, Nicholas?"

"Ask Sam or Trent. She fidgeted the whole time we talked with her. She was vague about her history. Did you even look at her résumé? Her life might as well have been nonexistent before she moved here." Nick moved to the window and rubbed his neck with his free hand. "The only thing I can check out is the fact she volunteered at the local animal shelter."

"See there, she does have experience with animals."

"Dogs and cats, not horses, pigs, or cows."

"Good enough for me. Honey, I'm sure she's just nervous; the four of you can be overwhelming. I have no doubt the scowl never left your face the whole time. As for her hiding something..." She sighed. "Aren't we all? We don't reveal the skeletons in our closets to a person we just met. I'm sure you didn't divulge any information about yourself."

"I'm not the one applying for a job." His voice rose out of frustration, and he closed his eyes. "I'm sorry."

"Nick, honey, you're suspicious of everyone around you. I love the fact you care for your brothers, but you need to let your guard down a bit. Let people in, sweetheart."

"Like Trent did?"

"No one knew his fiancée had mental issues."

"Which is why I planned on thoroughly investigating everyone who applied for this job—*before* we hired them."

"You're not responsible for April shooting your brother."

"Not directly." He rubbed his neck again. "We're getting off track. This has nothing to do with Darcy."

"It has everything to do with her."

"Ma, she doesn't even have a solid work history." He crossed the room and sat heavily on the couch. *But she does have a hot body.* One he found alluring along with her small rounded bottom, the tantalizing caramel color of her eyes, her plump bottom lip. Would it taste as good as it looked?

"She doesn't need one to clean cabins and scoop animal dung."

He shook off his wayward thoughts. "I don't trust her."

"There lies *your* problem. *I* think she's going to work out great. What was your brothers' reaction? Do they agree with you?"

If my brothers were as taken with her as I was, we're all in trouble.

He sighed and brought his full attention back around to the prospect of Darcy working on the ranch. "Doesn't matter. I'm the oldest, I overrule them." A small sense of satisfaction filled him.

"And *I* overrule you."

"Mom..."

"Nicholas, I hired her. You *will* show her the ropes and be nice to her."

Would she ever listen to him? Closing his eyes, he put his head on the back of the couch. "Fine, but if she screws up, she's out of here."

His mother breathed out noisily. "But you'll give her a fair chance and give her time to learn the ranch?"

"Yes."

"Good. Now don't sound glum, Nicky. Who knows, you might be surprised. We'll be in touch in a few days. I love you, honey."

"Love you, too." Nick punched the off button and tossed the phone on the couch, then shut his eyes. *Great.*

What had Darcy said to make his mother like her?

Not that he disliked her. As a female, he liked her, at least on an appearance level. Physically, her body possessed curves in the right places—not to mention her thick mass of curls and big bay eyes.

He should implement a dress code. No tight clothing.

Ha. His brothers would laugh him off the ranch. These long days were obviously getting to him. Now he'd lost his mind.

Nick jumped up. He would do well to avoid Miss Brooks and leave his family to handle her. She won't last longer than the week anyway.

"What'd Mom have to say?" Sam leaned on the door frame with arms crossed over his chest.

"She hired Darcy, and we're to show her the ropes." Nick crossed to the desk and made a project of organizing the papers. He stuffed the stapler into the top drawer and slammed the wood shut.

"Why are you against her working here?"

"You saw her. She couldn't sit still during the whole meeting. Her answers were evasive at best. I bet she's never even been to *Girard*." Why was he the only one who saw the problem here? Were they all blind?

"Shouldn't be too hard to check out." His brother moved to stand behind one of the chairs, his beefy hands resting on the wooden back. "Come on, she's a nervous thing, I'll give you that, but cut her some slack. I like her. She has a spark in her eye like she's ready to take on anything and everyone." He smiled and sat on the edge of the desk. "Including you."

Nick shook his head. "Something's not right. I can feel it."

"Ya, I bet you can." He chuckled. "Man, the stare

down between the two of you contained enough sparks for the Fourth of July."

Choosing to ignore the comment, Nick laid her papers out in front of him. "If you're too busy, have Chris or Trent show her Theresa's old cabin. She has today to get settled, but I want her at the barns by six a.m. tomorrow."

"Why can't you show her?" The second oldest grinned.

"I want to spend some time going over her information and calling her references." Nick scanned the pages without actually reading the print. He needed time to mull over the situation.

"Uh-huh. I'm sure that's it."

He frowned. "What's that mean?"

"Nothing."

Whistling, Sam got up from the desk and left the room.

****

By the next morning, Nick had failed to find anything out regarding one Darcy Brooks. Nor did he figure out what bothered him about her. He finished his coffee, placed his mug in the sink, and faced his brothers gathered for their regular morning meeting.

"I want you guys to show Darcy how to handle the smaller animals today."

"You workin' the horses today?" Chris questioned.

"Yes."

"Aren't you going to let Darcy help?" his youngest brother continued, pulling on his boots.

Chris remained the only Matthews living in the main house. The others occupied private cabins within the same vicinity of Darcy's. The decision to move into the cabins had been made when each brother turned twenty-one, craving privacy from one another *and* their parents. Something he could use right now.

"Not today." Nick waited for Trent to move out of the way before grabbing his hat and jamming it on.

"Need to get your head on straight before you work with her, huh?" Sam grinned and lifted his cup to his lips.

Nick glared in his direction then stomped out the door, letting the frame bang shut. He made his way across the ground, watching the sun rise far off in the distance.

Why did Darcy rattle him? What was she keeping from them?

He sighed. The fact he failed to contact one person last night who knew her personally reinforced his doubts. Too bad his mother didn't listen to him. Another burden lying on his shoulders.

Working through his frustrations, he stacked feed bags, grained the horses, filled water buckets, and mucked stalls. By ten, he hadn't seen nor heard from any of his brothers, and his shirt dripped with sweat. The ranch remained quiet from the human standpoint; the animals of course carried their own conversations.

He released the horses out to pasture and topped off the outside water tubs before going in search of the others.

Had Darcy showed up this morning? He bet she'd been late. He stopped at the cow barn and noted clean stalls.

Where is everyone?

Nick continued to the goats' feeding tub in the next barn. Big chunks of brown and tan filled the bucket.

What the hell?

He reached in, lifted a handful to his nose and sniffed. Unable to help himself, he chuckled. The tenderfoot had fed the goats *dog* food. He tossed the food back into the bin. She'd prove him right by the end of the week.

Ambling out of the barn, he started down the hill. What other animals had his brothers let her handle? A puttered *baa-baa* caught his attention to the right.

Damn the woman. She'd put the sheep in the bull pen. Now things were getting dangerous. Lucky for her the bulls weren't out...yet. Fisting his hands in irritation, he hurried his steps, sprinting around to the back. The gate to the deer run swung open in the slight breeze. He scanned left then right. *Who left the gate open?*

Suddenly, his gaze narrowed on the small object of destruction running around the horse pasture, two deer sprinting away from her. The antler-less animals advanced halfway down the field before stopping to graze, giving Darcy time to catch up.

Chris moved in from the side, holding out a handful of grain, but the four-legged creature was more interested in his shirttails hanging loose at his waist. *He knows better than to have his clothing loose.*

Darcy reached out to grab the animal, but the doe sprinted off before she gained hold. She stumbled into his youngest brother's chest, and the two tumbled into a pile of straw.

A slight breeze carried the sound of their laughter to Nick's ears. His fist clenched tight. What were they doing? This was no time for fun and games. He stomped closer, intending to break it up as the runt pushed himself to his feet and kicked the bedding at the new employee.

"Get those deer back in the pen!" he yelled, stopping their nonsense.

The pair jolted, and eyes so like his own narrowed in his direction as he closed the distance.

"Oh, hey, Nick. We had a problem with the deer."

"I can see that." He gritted his teeth. "What I want to know is why you're standing here laughing instead of getting them back where they belong."

Darcy's face paled. "I'm sorry. Don't be mad at Chris. It was my fault. He asked me to shut the gate."

"No. I forgot to tell you the latch sticks open." He laid a hand on her shoulder.

Nick looked from his brother's hand, to Darcy, then to the most immature Matthews's face. Suspicion ate at his gut and he narrowed his eyes. "I don't give a damn who's to blame. Get those deer back where they belong." He inhaled to ward off his rising blood pressure. "There's also the matter of moving the sheep from the pasture in front of the barn before Trent or Sam let the bulls out."

"What?" The squirt frowned.

Nick's sights settled on Darcy. "The sheep are in the bull pen."

She shifted from one foot to the other and wiggled her fingers. "Me again, I'm afraid."

Chris slapped his hat on his knee. "I should have specified what pasture."

"Go get those damn deer before they cause problems."

His brother hurried to corral the animals as one of the does headed into the horse barn.

Darcy started after him. "I'll go help."

"Not so fast." Nick caught her arm in his hand. Cool, smooth skin registered under his fingers. He slid a thumb over her bicep as he loosened his hold, fighting the urge to pull her closer. Raising his sights from her arm to her face, his muscles tightened at the spark of interest lighting her eyes.

"This is my fault. I should help him."

"I appreciate your honesty, but now that the does are in the horse barn, he won't have any trouble."

She frowned down to where his hand circled her thin arm. He let go.

"I know I messed up. I'll make sure I get it right tomorrow." Thin brows broke over expressive eyes. "Please don't fire me." Her chin lifted and tongue darted out to lick dry lips. "I love working with the animals. I'd never do anything to intentionally hurt them."

He swallowed, his anger subsiding with her plea. At least she appeared remorseful. Respect filled him. She owned up to her mistakes, not letting Chris take the blame. A funny sensation fluttered in his torso. He rubbed his chest.

Aw, hell. "I'm not going to fire you."

"Thank you." Relief shown on her face as she started forward. "I'll go move the sheep."

"There's also the problem in the goat barn."

Stopping, her brows and nose wrinkled in puzzlement.

How could he remain upset when she looked so damn cute? He pushed his hat back on his head. "Someone filled the tubs with dog food."

He bit back a chuckle at her frustrated groan.

"I keep Dakota's food up at the house. The bag must have gotten mixed up when Trent pulled the sacks of feed from the truck yesterday."

"I'll fix it right away."

Nick admired the sway of her hips as she scurried toward the barn. This morning's mix-ups presented the perfect opportunity to prove his point to the others *and* his mother, so why hadn't he fired Darcy on the spot?

Her embarrassed little smile flashed in his mind together with the way she jutted her chin out in stubbornness, and the impact hit him with lightning speed.

Damn. He was in trouble.

****

The next morning, Darcy scanned her living room as she pulled on her boots. Chris had called the one-story cabin small when he first warned her of the space. To her, the one bedroom, open living room, and kitchenette cabin was perfect. Everything she needed— dishes, towels, cupboards full with food. Her own place.

Making her way out the door, the sun peeked out from the horizon behind the buildings and a sense of peace surrounded her as she strolled to the barns.

Sam winked as she approached. "You look refreshed."

"How could I not feel energized breathing in all this fresh air?"

"Mornin'," Trent said in monotone from beside him.

"We missed ya at supper last night," the stockier of the two continued, his eyes shining bright. "You do know you're welcome to eat with us. Our cook, Ms.

Liz, makes enough to feed an army."

"Yes, thank you. But I was really tired." Guilt ate at her insides. Chris had informed her of the dinner arrangements, but after the mishaps yesterday, she dreaded facing Nick. When Chris declared her done for the day, she'd rushed to hide in her cabin with her strawberry jelly sandwich.

"Long as you know it's an open invitation."

"Thank you."

"Come on, we'll work on the cows again." Trent led the way to the cattle barn.

For the next hour, he helped her feed and water the milk animals. He spoke little, but when he did his voice was quiet and calming to even the most skittish animals. Sam, on the other hand, talked and laughed, filling her in on different animals and the bad behavior of a few as he helped her remove the soiled straw from the small herds' living quarters and replaced the bedding with new. Trent laughed a couple of times during the morning, but Darcy wondered what lurked in the shadows of his face.

About midmorning, Chris showed her the guest cabins before making their way to the goats. Not once during the course of chores did she see Nick.

He remained the one Matthews who made her question if she made the right decision taking the job. Who knew the difference between goat and dog food? Or the corral that connected to the sheep barn actually led to the bull pen. The fact remained, if she didn't improve, the top honcho was sure to have her head on a silver platter. Without Sam, Trent, and Chris, she'd have high-tailed her butt back to Jordan's by the end of her first day.

Stepping from the barn into the heat, Darcy fanned herself with a hand. The temperature had risen ten degrees in the past hour, but goose pimples rose on her arm. Feeling someone watching her, she swung her gaze around the surrounding area and turned in a circle. When a male body suddenly appeared beside her, she screeched and jumped back a foot.

"Ready for lunch?" Chris asked, taking off his gloves.

"You startled me," she admitted with a hand to her chest.

"I see that. Why so jumpy? Afraid Nick might be around?" He chuckled. "Don't let him bother you."

Easy for him to say.

Has Mr. Bossman been watching me? Waiting for me to screw up...again?

Darcy rubbed her arms, brushing off the sensation. She glanced to her watch. Past one. Must be the lack of substance making her delusional. "Food sounds great."

A small sense of worry found its way into her mind. What if Nick hadn't been watching? What if he was at the house? Her heart fluttered in her throat as she glanced around one more time as she mounted the steps.

Chris held the screen door open. "Want to help me move the pigs after we eat?"

"That's what I'm here for." She forced a smile as she passed him. If not for his easy nature, her lips were sure to fail at the attempt.

In the kitchen, a large woman stood with a scowl on her weathered features and a wooden spoon sticking out of the apron tied around her thick waist. "You're late."

"Sorry, Ms. Liz." Chris hung his hat on the rack before grabbing a plate and handing one to Darcy.

The cook gave a humph and moved to pour coffee. "The rest of the boys already ate and cleared out."

"We'll catch up." He piled his plate with cheese bread and homemade pizza before accepting a mug from her hand.

Darcy ducked around the forbidding woman who hurried out of the kitchen.

"Is she always so friendly?" She placed a slice of pizza on her plate and grabbed a cup of coffee before following the easy natured Matthews to the table in the corner of the kitchen.

"Ms. Liz means no harm. She isn't one for nonsense, and me being the jokester of the ranch put a burr in her bonnet years ago." He bit into his cheese bread. "She's really an okay woman, but runs a tight ship and expects us to follow her rules."

"It's your ranch."

"Yeah, but she's been here as long as I can remember. There's also the respecting-your-elders factor. My ma is big on manners and respect. If she couldn't brand it into our skull, my dad made sure he did."

Darcy sipped the caffeine and closed her eyes, her taste buds flooding with the rich flavor. "She does make some mean coffee."

"Best around." Chris stuffed pizza in his mouth, his warm hazel eyes sparkling with mischief. "Now, I should warn you about the pigs. Horace can get an attitude every now and again, but he means no harm."

She downed her java with a grimace. "I haven't handled the pigs yet. I'm sure you'll be entertained."

"You're doing great."

She gave a sarcastic laugh. He obviously suffered from short-term memory loss.

"I'm serious, Darcy."

Shaking her head, she watched him devour his food in haste and managed to get a few bites into her stomach. Chris finished in record time, and she drained the remains of her cup before following him to the pigs' pen.

"We need to get the sows from this pen into that one." He pointed to the enclosed area not four feet away and opened the gate for her to enter.

"Are you sure that pen's not for the goats or deer?" She squinted in the sun's rays. "There isn't one an acre away or anything?"

Chris smirked and his eyes softened. "Come on, Darcy. You'll get the hang of everything."

"You're right. Sorry." *Toughen up, girl.*

"Glad you agree. Now, we need to move the pigs in order to improve the drainage. Horace is digging too deep into the ground. If we don't fix the problem, he'll dig his way out of the enclosure." He chuckled. "He likes to escape any chance he gets."

Great. Just what she needed—a pig on the loose. *Horace the Troublemaker.* She made a mental note, eyeing the mischievous livestock.

Extracting the rubber band from her hair, she pushed the run-away strands back, and retied her unruly curls at the base of her neck. "What's the game plan?"

"Anyway that works."

His smile grew contagious, and her spirits lifted. She liked working with Chris. He kept things light. No pressure.

"Uh-oh."

She twisted around in time to see Nick approaching, glowering in her direction.

Chapter Three

Darcy stepped back. "He doesn't look happy."

Chris's lean form bent toward her. "Probably swallowed a fly or something."

She hid a giggle behind her hand.

Nick frowned at his brother. The muscle in his cheek worked at a steady pace. "You're supposed to be helping Trent with the sheep."

"Sam's in town picking up a load of rock for the pen and asked me to move the pigs before he gets back. Darcy agreed to help."

"Head down and help Trent. I'll help her move the pigs." Broad shoulders stiffened as he stepped into the fenced area, his eyes not straying from his sibling.

Chris stared back, appearing ready to say something. Tension snapped through the air like a crackle in a stormy gray sky, and Darcy bit her lip to keep from telling Nick he was being awfully hard on his youngest brother.

The kinder one shook his head and left, brushing his shoulder against his elder.

The brute sighed and turned. "You ready?"

She stuck out her chin and firmed up her lips. "Yes." Though annoyed with the way he treated his brother, his standoffish attitude kept her on edge. Not to mention his downright unapproachable appearance with his black Stetson pulled low, and the black shirt stretched taunt across his chest, tucked into his low-riding Wranglers.

She pulled on the neckline of her T-shirt. Working with Chris, she experienced a sense of calmness, but with this one...

Get your mind off your boss and on your job. She wiped her hands on her jeans. "Let's get started."

With the Almighty One's help, five of the seven pigs where relocated from one enclosure to the other. The last two proved more difficult. Darcy went one way, Nick another, only to circle back around and hit heads leaving her dizzy. Then the thick-headed animal led her around the maddening cowboy's legs causing her to slip. Her boots and jeans ended up covered in mud.

With a heavy breath, she pivoted just as Horace ran behind her, pushing her knees in. Someone squealed as she splattered hands first into the mud.

Oh man, what a mess.

Flinging the sludge from her fingers, she glared where Horace munched on the food remaining in his feed tub.

"This means war, *pig*." She pushed to her feet and wiped her hands on her thighs.

"Don't take your eye off him. He likes to play, especially in the mud," Nick told her as he corralled Charlotte toward the gate.

At the last minute, the sow twisted to one side and got away from him. Darcy eyed the unyielding monsters and advanced, pushing Charlotte's back end until she headed toward the opening. Then the pig stopped dead.

"Go on, join your friends." She shoved, but the darn animal stood her ground.

Come on, don't make me look bad.

"Be persistent. Don't back down." Nick wedged himself between the two. "If you let up, she'll hide by Horace."

Easy for him to say.

Planting her feet in the mud, Darcy pressed forward. After several long minutes, the swine conceded and joined the others.

Now for Horace the Troublemaker.

She pondered over a strategy, but came up empty. Deciding to wing it, Darcy approached with arms spread wide. Nick moved on the other side, while she angled her direction to shove Horace to the left. But the slippery swine veered and ran behind her legs.

Damn it.

This pig was getting the best of her, and in front of her boss to boot. She needed to make him move, to prove she wasn't completely incompetent.

Foot glopped in mud, she circled him. He sprinted to the right, and her hand scraped against the thick skinned menace. Horace squealed and moved to the left faster than she believed the fat hog capable. Wiping her brow with the back of her arm, she lunged to catch him, missing by inches and fell face first into the mud.

Spitting and sputtering the dirt from her lips, she lifted her head in time to see Horace strut in front of her, sticking his pink nose in the air before strutting through to the other pen.

No way.

Darcy rolled over, breathing hard from the unexpected exercise. She flung a forearm over her eyes to block out the sight of Nick peering over her.

"You okay?"

Removing the barrier, she witnessed a twitch of his lips beneath the thin layer of scruff covering his jaw.

"Thanks for all your help." *Not.* Other than standing there, he hadn't done a thing to help with Horace.

He held a hand out to her. "Looked like you had him under control."

Darcy rose onto her elbows. *Yuck.* Her jeans were caked with who knew what else. Anxious to get out of the stench, she placed her hand in his. Palm to palm, her heart skipped a beat, and she forgot to breath.

He tugged on her arm, pulling her to her feet. His arm went around her waist as she slammed into his chest. The unexpected heat of him made her step back into one of Horace's holes, knocking them both off balance.

Nick twisted, bracing her against his hard chest as they landed back in the muck. Air whooshed from her lips. She stared at his mud-splattered form in horror.

Oh, God, he's sure to fire me now.

"I'm so sorry. Are you okay?" She tugged her foot to free it, catching her boot on the cuff of his jeans.

"I would be if you'd stop kicking me." All movement halted on her part as she stared, biting her bottom rim to keep from laughing as she wiped the specks from his cheek, making the damage ten times worse. His skin was warm and bristly under her finger, and she quickly withdrew her hand.

His chest rumbled beneath her.

Startled by the warmth that spread through her, she levitated herself by placing her palms on his chest.

"You should see yourself." His lips lifted at the corners before he broke out in a full laugh.

A second later she joined him. "Me? What about you?"

His thumb wiped a clump of sludge off her check as he moved his leg. Every hard inch of him pressed into her flesh, branding her to him.

When he tucked a stray curl behind her ear, a spark ignited in her toes and heat worked through her body. His chest rose and fell in a rapid pace beneath her palms, but her own air suspended in her lungs. She fought a wild urge to rake a fingernail over his unshaved jaw.

She sucked in a breath. This was not right. The way her body succumbed to one touch of his hand was wrong.

Darcy pulled her knees up in an effort to get to her feet. Large hands encased the back of her thighs in a stilling motion, and she ending up straddling him as he rose to a sitting position. A helpless gasp robbed her of speech and pulled his eyes to her lips.

She gave herself a mental shake and swallowed the moan rising in her throat. Ripples of anticipation churned deep inside, and she forced herself to look away. The magnificent body was off limits. *He's my employer for goodness sake.*

"I—I must look quite a sight," she commented, trying to escape her own thoughts.

"We both do." He smirked, revealing a devilish indentation in his left cheek.

When did he get a dimple? She didn't remember seeing one before.

Muscles flexed under her and the heat of him

seeped through her jeans. She glanced away, wondering how to talk her jelly-filled muscles into getting up. Failing to persuade her body, her sights returned to his. Green specks highlighted his brown orbs—a*nother new finding to keep the breath from my lungs.*

"We, uh, should get cleaned up."

His voice broke through her muddled brain. Nodding, one by one she convinced her limbs to move and scrambled to her feet before he attempted to help her again. "Where exactly can we do that?"

"There's a hose by the barn." He picked his hat up out of the muck as he rose and led the way.

The wooden structure loomed not far ahead and as much as she wanted the goop out of her hair, she stayed a couple of paces back because her nerve endings sizzled when she got too close.

Wonderful. Not only did she have to worry about screwing up the job, now she had to find a way to rein in suddenly uncontrollable hormones.

Nick cursed under his breath the whole way to the barn. He was right in keeping his distance from Darcy yesterday. Too bad his judgment failed him today. While he found her mishaps slightly amusing, he grew worried over her safety. Yet, though the animals got the better of her on occasion, she never quit and continued to tend to the rebellious creatures with a caring hand. He admired her spunk and determination more than he wished to admit.

Running a hand threw his muddy hair, he fought the desire to turn around and haul her into his arms again. At thirty-two, he figured himself capable of controlling his urges. What he hadn't counted on was the intensity of the pull. His body had responded to her in a millisecond when she landed on top of him, and he'd wanted more than his next breath to raise his head and kiss those luscious lips.

He groaned inward, recalling the way her breasts pushed on the pale green cotton shirt tucked into the small waistband of her jeans. She'd turned his blood hot with one glance. *Damn.*

Nick grasped the hose and twisted the nozzle, spraying his face with cold water. The blast knocked the air right out of him. Nothing like a cold shower and a dose of priorities to get his mind straight.

He held the hose over his head and doused his heated body. Monday needed to get here fast. The business meetings he'd set up out of town should help snap his hormones back into place. The magazine companies who agreed to meet with him were widely known and great advertisement for the ranch. Many folks were interested in vacationing at a dude ranch, and his job was to convince the families to vacation at the *Matthews* Dude Ranch. The business was a whole lot safer to think about than the body standing next to him.

He shook the water from his hair, rinsed his arms, and opened his eyes to find Darcy not two feet from him. Even with clumps of mud in her hair and smudged on her face she was a sight of beauty.

"Your, uh..." His voice croaked like a gangly teenager. He forced his throat to clear and, raising the hose, stepped toward her. "Your turn."

At the first blast of the water, her eyes widened and a gasp escaped her lips. She laughed and tipped her head to pull out the band securing her hair. Slender fingers ran through the curls as she bent forward giving him a clear view of her cleavage.

Nick followed the contour of her body and all but groaned out loud. Her nipples hardened before his eyes, and he imagined rolling the tight beads in his fingertips. His body tightened at the provocative image.

When she lifted her hair and turned, the water cascaded down her back to her firm, tight ass.

He sucked in a breath. Lusting after an employee was *not* one of his better ideas, but he couldn't turn away.

Rotating in a circle, she stopped and stared in his direction. A piece of him melted. Surely, those big brown eyes could buy her the moon. His feet shuffled closer even as his brain told him to stop. He touched the side of her face.

"You missed a spot." Using the side of his wet thumb, he rubbed the dirt off her cheek. As expected, her cool skin was smooth and soft.

When she licked her lips, he zeroed in on the movement. Adrenaline rushed through him. Unable to stop himself, he tucked her hair behind her ear and noted the pulse twitched at the base of her throat. His free hand found its way to the back of her neck, nudging her closer. The hose fell out of his other hand as the thought of tasting her had his mouth lowering to hers.

Cold water spurted up between them and Nick sprang back, noting through the frozen mist that the hose had landed on the trigger of the sprayer. He grabbed the handle ceasing the shower of water.

Darcy blinked, then doubled over in a fit of laughter. The sound contagious, he soon found himself chuckling, too, realizing he had never enjoyed a day's work quite this much.

Suddenly she straightened in haste and looked around, her doe eyes round as saucers. Rubbing her wet arms with her hands, she whipped her head from one direction to the other.

Alarm set in. "What's wrong?"

"I heard something." She scanned the area, appearing ready to bolt into hiding.

"Probably one of the animals."

She shook her head. "No, it sounded like someone said my name." Her sights darted around for whatever sound she heard.

He glanced to the right then the left, but saw no one.

"I didn't hear anything." Why was she so skittish?

"G-guess just my imaginations working overtime."

"Uh-huh. Care to explain why?"

Nick watched her rewrap the band around her hair with shaky movements. The way she jumped from one extreme to the next, just like April, bothered him. He needed a way to figure out what she hid from him.

"Too much sun." Her lips lifted in an attempt to smile, but fell short as her gaze took in the surroundings again.

If not for the way her fingers curled into a tight fist, he might have believed her. "Why don't you head on down to the guest cabins. They need cleaned before the next group arrives. The supplies should be in the closet in cabin one." *While I take time to sort this all out before I make a complete mess of my life.*

She grimaced at her clothes. "Would it be okay if I change first?"

"Sure." Nick watched her saunter away, which was

becoming an addicting hobby, one sure to bite him in the ass. Her head moved back and forth as she scanned the area then glanced his way before hurrying off.

He scouted the vicinity, half hoping to see anything to validate her actions. Maybe he'd try to get a hold of her friend again tonight. Last night, all he got was an answering machine. Tomorrow, he'd have Darcy work with him in the horse barn. If he talked to her alone, she might shed some light on her past. Not to mention, the bonus of splitting Chris and her up. The way those two carried on, it was a wonder anything got done.

He glanced around at the mess. Then again, maybe he should fire her before anything more happened. His mother would understand his safety concerns. If not, he'd make her see reason. The woman proved harmful to the ranch...and his libido.

****

"I'm gonna call Mom tonight and tell her this isn't working," Nick informed his brothers at supper that evening.

"What's not?" Trent stuffed some meatloaf in his mouth.

"Darcy."

"It's only been two days. Give her time." Sam put his fork down and stood, stretching his back.

"And in those forty-eight hours, she's caused more chaos than the Miller's five kids last month." Nick gulped his coffee. Five naughty boys ranging in ages from eight to fifteen ran amuck around the grounds, going in and out of every stall, pen, and cage at any given hour. The parents let the monstrous five come and go as they pleased with no regards to the rules.

"Give her time to get her bearings. Geeze, not

everyone's perfect. You certainly aren't," Chris huffed. "Maybe if you'd take time to be around her, you'd see how hard she's trying." His eyes narrowed, and his lip snarled.

"Don't give me that look, Christopher. You're partly to blame."

"For what? Having fun?" He tossed his napkin down. "You need to lighten up. You haven't even tried to make her feel comfortable."

Oh hell. If he *felt* anymore of her, she'd be filing a sexual harassment charge. He jabbed his fork into another piece of meat.

"Mom hired her to do a job, not goof off. Maybe if you two spent more time concentrating on what needed done, she'd figure out how to care for the animals without mayhem."

"She does do her job!" His voice rose. "But any time she spots you coming, she gets nervous. And can you blame her? You could try being nicer."

Nick eyed his brother's defensive glare. A pang of jealousy over Chris and Darcy's bond gnawed his gut.

"I am nice to her."

"No, you're not. You flipped out on her for mixing up the feed and a broken gate latch. Even at the pig pen, you jumped down our throats. Try being her friend instead of a tyrant." The youngest brother chugged his water.

"Is that what you are, her friend?" He'd wondered over the relationship since he happened upon them corralling the deer, kicking hay at each other. "I'm gonna tell you right now, you may be twenty-one, but I'll kick your ass if you sleep with Darcy, or any other future employee on this ranch," he added quickly.

"What? You're nuts." The inexperienced runt threw his fork down. "I can have female friends without having sex. Unlike you. Maybe it's *you* who is attracted to her."

No way. He stood, the chair flipping back in his haste.

Sam's hand closed over Nick's arm. He inhaled and released the air slowly. *Why was Chris jumping to her defense?*

"What's up with the two of you?"

"I'm fine," he lied, as the jealousy reared its ugly head.

The realization struck him square in the chest. He half expected Chris to put a fist to his face. Guilt ate at him. He blamed his blood relation for what he desired.

"Enough," Trent growled. "We promised not to let another woman come between us."

Nick blew out a breath. His brother was right. It'd been enough with Trent's fiancée and manipulative ways.

"Come on." Trent rolled his neck, cracking the bones. "We have to pull together and run this ranch for Mom and Dad's sake."

Chris pointed in Nick's direction. "I'm sick of it being his way or no way."

"Do *you* have feelings for Darcy?" Sam questioned Chris.

"She's just a friend. A good friend...and a hard worker. She makes work fun. I don't want her to leave."

Nick observed his youngest brother. Babied by his mother—in truth, by the whole family—he didn't act like a twenty-one-year-old, at least not the way any of them had acted...and he didn't have many friends. Hell, life on the ranch didn't allow for much social time.

He sighed. "I'll put off speaking to Mom about Darcy, for now."

Chris nodded, dropped his dishes in the sink, and stormed out.

"I'll go talk to him." Trent grabbed his cowboy hat and followed him outside.

The gap between him and his immature brother grew bigger every day, and he had no idea what caused it or how to fix the problem. He closed his eyes and rubbed a hand down his face. A chair slid on the wooden floor.

"You wanna tell me what's going on?" Sam leaned forward, resting his forearms on his thighs. "You don't usually let him get under your skin."

"I leave day after tomorrow for my advertising stint. I'm supposed to speak with the president of the magazine companies in Abilene, Pueblo, Wichita, and Tulsa. I have brochures to print and distribute. I have enough meetings and dinners in the surrounding cities to keep me away for a good month." He rubbed his neck, feeling tension grab hold of his muscles. "I just want to make sure the ranch runs properly while I'm away."

"Trips never bothered you before." He smiled. "Or is it Darcy chafing your ass?"

He shook his head. "I'm not comfortable leaving a new employee, who I know is hiding something, with the three of you."

"We're big boys; I'm sure we can handle her."

"Like Trent handled April?"

He sat back in his seat. "That's what this is about?

Nick, Darcy's not nuts."

"How do you know?"

"You read her physical exam. Nowhere did it say bipolar or even suggest a mental illness."

He shook his head, still not convinced.

"Look in her eyes. She doesn't have the crazy look April got when she didn't get her own way."

His lips lifted a fraction. He *had* looked in her eyes—too close. The big brown orbs sucked him in and left him gasping for air.

The second eldest grinned. "Admit it. The problem is you're attracted to her."

Too much. But he'd be damned if he'd admit it. Instead, he crossed to the sink. "I don't know her enough to say one way or the other."

His sibling followed on his heels. "You want to though, get to know her, I mean."

Nick's shoulders tightened as he leaned on the counter.

"Ever think you need a break from traveling? I mean, you only got back last month from the conference in Montana."

"Maybe after this one."

"Why don't you let me go? That way you can stay and make sure Darcy learns the ropes."

"No. This is the part of the business I agreed to take on." While Sam went to school to learn the ins and outs of business and accounting, Nick found the traveling end of the ranch suited him. Until now...

"I'll go this time. A couple of weeks away might do me good."

"No. It's my responsibility. I'll go. Just do me a favor and make sure Chris and Darcy remain platonic while I'm gone."

The self-appointed therapist's upper lip twitched. "For his sake, or yours?"

"Sam..." He gritted his teeth.

"Just askin'." Large hands rose in the air in an innocent gesture. "You can trust us to handle the ranch, you know? Even Darcy."

Nick pushed off the counter. "Yeah, but I'm the big brother. Humor me."

While he was away, he'd keep making calls until he found someone who could tell him more about one Miss Darcy Brooks.

"Hi, am I too late for supper?" The object of discussion opened the screen door and entered. With her came the fresh scent of a meadow full of flowers.

He closed his lids for a split second and inhaled. Never had a woman taken his breath away just by walking into the room. His taste buds watered at the sight of her. His gut tightened as blood surged to every nerve ending in his body. After everything he preached to Chris, he worried over his own reaction. His eyes snatched in each detail of her skin. The long hours working outside already tanned her upper body to a healthy glow, her small perky nose red on the rim. The light in the kitchen picked up the sun-streaked highlights in her brandy-colored curls as she moved through the room.

"Not at all. Ms. Liz keeps the food warm until eight." Sam grabbed a plate and handed it to her. "There's meatloaf in this pan, mashed potatoes in the one down there, and vegetables in the middle dish."

A brow raised in his direction. Nick knew his brother questioned his silence, but couldn't organize one intelligible sentence in his muddled brain.

"Thanks. Do you have any strawberry jelly?"

"Pardon?"

"You mean you've never put jelly on your meatloaf?"

The accommodating activist opened the refrigerator. "No." His chuckled filled the air.

"You should try it. It's really good." Darcy grasped the jar he held out and glanced at Nick. "I'm sorry I messed up yesterday."

Her gaze trapped him within the depths. "You're learning. It's expected."

Sam coughed, and Nick glowered at his brother.

"I'll try harder. I promise."

He cleared his throat and shrugged. "Meet me in the horse barn in the morning."

Hurrying toward the door before he made an ass out of himself, Nick snatched his hat off the rack, only to catch his brother following Darcy to the dining room.

"Mind if I sit with you while you eat? I can answer any questions you have regarding the ranch."

The pompous ass.

He slammed the door and headed out to do chores, hoping the manual labor would curb his frustrations.

Chapter Four

At sunup, Darcy made her way to the barn and slowed as she neared the buildings. Her nerves ate at her insides since she'd left her uneaten supper last night. She'd pushed the food around on her plate while Sam filled her in on the different animals, but not a minute of the conversation sunk in. Nick's cold, unwelcoming behavior, coupled with the uneasy feeling of someone watching her, filled her with anxiety.

Even now, goose-bumps rose on her skin. System on full alert, she scanned the surroundings while making her way across the makeshift road between her cabin and the barns. Even though the sun started coming up from the east, she found it difficult to spot anything out of the ordinary in the distance. On the upside, she didn't get the same eerie feeling as the day before.

Entering the horse barn, she noted the second object of her anxiety working in one of the stalls. Darcy smoothed the front of her short-sleeve, pale pink T-shirt and took a shaky breath. "Hi."

Nick's head popped over the wooden door for a split second. "Mornin'. Grab the pitch fork off the wall and come in."

She collected the equipment he indicated and made her way back to the stall.

"I already grained the horses and put them out to pasture."

"Am I late?" She glanced to her watch. No, six o'clock on the dot.

"I started early." He angled the wheelbarrow out of the way for her to enter. His gray shirt stretched the seams with his movements. "This shouldn't take too long. When we're done, I'll show you where we keep the horse feed."

"You sure you trust me to feed the horses after the goat incident?" Plunging the end of the rake into the soiled material, she scooped the manure and placed the waste in the wheelbarrow.

"It's easier if you scrape the sawdust into a pile before scooping." He leaned on the shovel. "You'll get the hang of things if you stop doubting yourself. If I make up charts of who gets what grain and how much, do you think it would help?"

"Yes. And if you have the vet on speed dial that would help." She drew the sawdust closer and pivoted with the weighted-down shovel. The end hit the wall, landing a few droppings in the water pail. Darcy shut her eyes and groaned, then peeked at Nick who stood motionless, his jaw clenched.

He lifted the urine-soaked dust. "We'll clean the bucket out when we're finished."

Loosen up. Relax. The simplest task, picking up crap, and she mucked it up.

Mucked it up. She giggled, obviously too many days spent dwelling on her shortcomings were getting to her.

"Want to let me in on the joke?" Frowning, his eyes narrowed in her direction.

"Nervous energy. Sorry." Sweat dotted her brow, and she swiped at the moisture with the back of her hand.

He ceased all movement and frowned. "Because of me?"

"Yep." Might as well put her cards on the table. If she continued to mess up, she'd make sure he knew her downfall resulted because of him.

Seconds ticked by; she forced herself not to look up and continue with her chore. When a hand gripped her shoulder, she froze. Her heart thumped hard in her ears as she slowly gazed up.

Nick's lips lifted, and a sharp bolt of desire hit her. *Killer smile, who knew?* She glanced away from his alluring mouth.

A finger under her chin turned her head toward him, and she held her breath.

"I don't mean to make you edgy. I want you to be relaxed." His brows dipped around his green-brown gaze as he dropped his hand to his side. "The way you are around my brothers."

Oxygen became a must, and she sucked in the much needed air in small, quick gasps. Nick wanted her to joke around with him? A bubble of amusement swirled in her belly. He'd have to get a sense of humor for that to happen.

No. That wasn't fair. He had laughed with her over the incident in the pig pen.

"Never mind. Let's get this done. I want to see how you do grooming the horses."

And just like that, the moment passed. Though she didn't know what to make of his Jekyll and Hyde personality, Darcy grew excited at the prospect of handling the equines. The large creatures had drawn her interest from the first day.

After dumping and filling the water bucket, he motioned to her. "Follow me. I want to introduce you to T.J."

He walked through a middle aisle and turned to the first stall. Exhilaration filled her at the sight of the animal waiting to join his friends.

The horse stretched his head toward her, and she stroked his muzzle. "He's beautiful."

"Glad you think so, 'cause he's yours to ride while you work here."

"What?" Her head snapped back raising her sights to his. Did she even know how to ride?

Oh, boy, I've really got myself into a mess now.

"You do know how to ride, don't you?" His mouth set in a grim line.

She inhaled the hay/animal scents and a sudden light-headedness made her lean on the wood—a vision of laughing and running through a pasture with a horse hooked to the end of a lead rope floated across her stark mind. A sense of right flowed over her. She shut her eyes to capture the fleeting image.

"Darcy?"

Popping her lids open, she swallowed and bit her trembling rim until she tasted blood. "I..."

"Stop." Nick held up a hand. "Let me guess, you applied for a job on a ranch, but you don't know how to ride, is that about the gist of it?"

Her cheeks grew warm as she lowered her chin. "I...I rode when I was younger." She shifted her weight and kicked the dung off her boot, hoping he trusted her words. If she didn't believe her own declaration, how could he? But...was that really a memory or only wishful thinking?

Squaring her shoulders with a strange new confidence, she met his gaze and nodded.

He rubbed his neck and sighed. "We'll have a refresher course then, but not now. Today, I want you and T.J. to get acquainted, do a couple rounds of ground work together." He crossed to the tack room and came back a minute later with a halter and rope dangling from his fingertips.

Holding the vision as something real she prayed, *Please let me know what I'm doing.* A lump of uncertainty formed in her chest. Up until now, the chores she tackled held no real danger, but a horse...the creature possessed more strength than the smaller animals.

"First, we're going to put him in cross ties, then I want you to groom him. Afterward, we'll get him saddled and work with him in the corral." A large hand held the halter out.

Pushing her doubts aside, she focused on the horse as she moved to his stall. Her hand stroked the side of T.J.'s neck. Calmness flowed through her veins. She placed the gelding's nose through the nylon, slid it up his face and secured the buckle. The action seemed familiar and right. She stroked the animal, and a sense of serenity swept over her. Clipping the lead rope under his chin, she brought him to the center of the barn.

Nick grinned. "Just like riding a bike, right?"

She smiled, but wasn't sure if it was because of the notion of her memory coming back, or because of his approval.

He attached the lines to the rings on the wall and

gave a tug. "That should do. I have a few things to check on while you get started." He handed her a container filled with the equipment. "He's all yours."

She turned toward the horse. Her hand closed around the comb in the caddy. Bringing the teeth to T.J.'s mane, she struggled with the knots. Another sense of familiarity washed through her and she swayed backward, shaking her head. Tentatively, she stepped back to the horse, touching his face with the bristles.

The palomino lowered his head and angled toward her, pushing into her hand.

The brush fell from her fingers as a sudden mental picture of combing another horse at another time filtered in from the cobwebs of her mind. Trembling, she reached up and scratched behind his ears.

"Look at this patch of hair you have tangled." Afraid if she stopped moving she might think too hard, Darcy picked up the brush at her feet and used the teeth on the strands hanging down his face.

Her fingers worked through the mass until they slid through with ease. "One more side."

The instrument traveled from his withers to his rump, from his back to each leg. She brushed his back, sides, and belly. Dust filled the air, making her cough. She came around to his face. Brown orbs regarded her and...

"Look how clean he is. You did a good job, kiddo." A dark-haired man smiled down at her.

"Thank you."

"You're going to take real good care of him, I'm sure of it. You wanna start working with him now?"

"I'd love to, if you have the time."

"For you, of course."

"Darcy?"

She jumped and put her hand to her chest as Nick came into her visual. "Y-you scared me."

A worried frown marked his face. "I called your name, twice."

"I wasn't paying attention." With a grimace, she veered away.

"Uh-huh." A tan hand smoothed over the gelding's rump. "Hand me the pick. I'll get his hooves clean while you get the black saddle and pad off the rack in the tack room."

Darcy scurried away to retrieve the equipment and embrace the mental images circling her head.

All this time she waited and waited for something, anything. Why now? Her body shook with mixed emotions. Who was the man? And why did she get a warm feeling at the memory? What did it all mean?

Funny how months ago she longed to recall her life, now the idea of remembering caused an emotional uproar. The notion of recalling her past both delighted and scared the daylights out of her. What if her past took her from the present, the life she worked hard to create?

The terror over Nick discovering her amnesia bore too much for her to concentrate. Would he fire her on the spot? She closed her eyes and pulled oxygen deep into her lungs before rejoining him.

"I'm going to assume you don't know how to saddle him and show you." The cowboy relieved her of the heavy gear. "Unless you're sure you can."

"You go ahead. I'll watch." She breathed in and out.

"No. You're going to help me." He placed the

saddle on the stall wall. "Here. Put the pad up on his withers."

She snatched the cushion from his fingers and placed the cushion across T.J.'s back. The horse shifted, his belly pushing her backward into the solid wall of Nick's chest.

Her teeth bit into her tongue to keep from moaning at the impact.

"Don't let him crowd you." A large hand reached around her and put pressure on the gelding's side until he moved out of her space.

"Leave the pad up in the air." He adjusted the material. "When you tighten the girth, it compresses down."

A saddle appeared in front of her. Lost in her own turmoil, she mechanically moved, taking the seat from him to heave up over the gelding's back.

Her arm bumped into solid muscles on her right. Fingers closed around her bicep.

"Sorry."

His lips lifted a fraction as he rotated the stirrups. "This is the cinch." He grabbed the strap under the horse's belly. "Make sure it's straight, nothing's bunched, or twisted. This rope—" He took hold of another strap and motioned with his hands. "Put it through the metal loop of the cinch, up through this ring twice."

Grasping the end, she concentrated on the instructions.

"Now, loop it." Strong fingers covered hers. His chest pressed to her back. "Go around the metal and down through."

The deep voice vibrated down to her toes. Hot

breath ruffled her hair, and her stomach tightened. The urge to close her lids and rest her head on him surged hard.

"Let's walk him out of the barn. He'll be ready to tighten by the time we get him to the corral."

Missing the closeness of his body, Darcy followed his sinful form out into the warm sun. A light wind tousled the strands of hair escaping her short ponytail, and she shoved the stubborn locks back.

"This is how you tighten the strap." Sure fingers pulled up on the line. "Make sure you secure the end before you mount up. Otherwise your saddle may slip to the side."

"Tighten before you ride. Got it."

"I'm going to help you work him. I wanna see how you do with lunging."

"Okay." Her tummy rolled.

"I wanted to show you the trails tomorrow, but the cabins need finished and—"

"They shouldn't take me long. There are only two left to clean."

"...and I have to go out of town for a couple of weeks."

"You're leaving?" she asked in a small voice when she realized they'd spoken over each other.

He paused and gave a slight tilt of his head. "I have meetings with some advertising companies to help bring more business."

Not sure if she was relieved or upset over his departure, she focused out in the distance.

"I should only be gone for a couple of weeks. When the next big group arrives, I want you to go on the overnighter. We take the vacationers to a designated area in the woods where we camp and cook out. These people have been here before and want to head out right away.

"When are they due in?"

"Not for another three weeks. That should give you enough time to get your bearings. There're smaller gatherings scheduled between now and then, but not for the camping experience." His lips set in a grim line. "I'm not sure if I'll be here or not, but one of my brothers will be with you."

Not sure what to make of the information he divulged, she nodded.

"This will be the saddle you use whenever you ride."

Her horse. Her saddle. Her home. She was finally making a new life with new memories. She straightened her spine.

Nick handed the lunge line to her and led the way to the corral. Opening the gate, he motioned her to precede him. He shut the entry and leaned his tall muscular form on the fence.

"Walk him around a bit."

With the horse building her confidence with each step, Darcy gave her lungs the right to oxygen in slow steady breaths, letting the calming effect wash over her.

"Stand in the center."

Nick's baritone voice tingled down her back as he followed her to the sanded area. The heat from his body absorbed into her as he stood close behind. A calloused hand closed over hers, dissolving her strength into a puddle.

"Twirl this end. It will help to get him moving. Then take this hand—" His fingers slid down her arm causing her legs to turn to jelly. "And point the way you want him to go."

T.J. started off, and Nick let go.

Caught off guard at his sudden absence, she stepped back and collided with Nick's chest.

His hands went to her waist steadying her.

Her heart fluttered with the contact, but she set the feeling aside to step forward and point with the rope.

The animal started one way then reared to turn the other way.

"You're confusing him. Point with the hand *not* holding the line." Tepid fingers closed around her wrist. "Step out and look to his butt." He pulled her arms to her belly.

Darcy did as instructed. With his body guiding her movements, her nerve endings shorted out, zapping her senses to full capacity.

The horse stopped, more from Nick's body language than hers. Her mind, too busy absorbing the strength of the body wrapped around her, refused to focus on the exercise.

He raised her right arm, stuck her forefinger out and twirled the lead in her left, her arms performing as an extension of his own.

T.J. jumped and moved right.

"There ya go. Now stop him and turn him the other way." The cowboy let go and stepped back.

She missed the connection in an instant. Not having time to dwell, she focused on the horse, and soon had him moving in the direction she indicated.

"Good. Keep him going."

The relentless instructor guided her through for an hour before he called a halt.

"That's enough for today. You did real good and catch on quick." He smiled.

Her head tilted as she embraced the praise and tried to pull the vague memory to the surface.

"You can take him in the back and hose him down." He went on to instruct her on how to cool the horse. "Then put him out to pasture."

Needing time to think, to get her hormones under control, she sauntered to the barn.

Chapter Five

The day after Nick left, Darcy finished work later than usual and longed for a soak in the tub. She had just submerged her aching muscles into the hot bath when her cell phone rang.

Drying her hand, she placed the device to her ear. "Hello?"

"Hi, it's Nick."

Goose pimples rose on her skin despite the warm water and her eyes closed. He didn't need to tell her; she recognized his voice the second he spoke. *But why is he calling me?* "Is something wrong?"

"Not that I know of." A deep chuckle filled her ear. "Unless my brothers left you on your own?"

Funny how without him glaring down at her the comment made light of her mishaps. "Should I be insulted?" she chided back.

"No," he sighed. "I told Sam I'd check in on things, but no one answered."

"Trent and Chris went into town. I think Sam was headed for the shower." She raised her knees causing water to slosh over the side of the tub.

"What's that?"

"I'm...ah...water."

"It's kind of late to be watering the animals. They should have been fed and watered hours ago." Irritation lined his tone.

"Um, I'm not. I mean, they were."

"Are you doing dishes?"

"No."

"Well, the only other place you'd have water would be in the bath."

She sank deeper in the tub as if he could see her.

"Darc, are you in the—are you naked?" His voice choked.

"Yes." How else did one wash?

He let out what sounded like a groan. "I have to go."

The phone went silent. Tossing her cell onto the towel, she stuck her tongue out at the device. "If you didn't want to know, you shouldn't have asked."

She finished her bath in record time with the sound of Nick's groan circling her head.

He called two more times during the first week of his travels, short conversations, but on the third call, she ventured to ask his advice on how to deal with a couple of the animals.

"For the more stubborn ones, make sure you have a treat. It'll make for a lot less headaches in the end."

She sat up in her bed, adjusting the pillows behind her back. "What if I give the animal the wrong treat?"

He chuckled. "There's a possibility."

"Hey!" She laughed, then sobered when he remained silent.

"I like hearing you laugh." His hoarse voice deepened.

Playing with a loose string on the bed spread, she admitted, "It's easier to talk to you on the phone."

"I apologize if I haven't made things easy for you.

I'm glad you're more at ease with me now."

"It's a lot less painful when you're not staring at me with your brows bent over your eyes."

He chuckled, a deep rich sound.

She snuggled down into the bed. "I like hearing you laugh too."

Nick cleared his throat. "There are, ah, peppermints for the horses in the tack room," he said, picking up the previous conversation. "Roughage is in the refrigerator in the pig barn. For the others, grab a handful of feed from the bins."

"Thank you for the advice."

"Sleep well, Darc," he murmured.

The conversations with Nick helped her grow more secure in her decision to remain on the ranch. No other visions of her past surfaced. No other incidents occurred. No more feelings of someone watching her.

During the day, she stayed busy learning the ways of the ranch. She educated the guests' children on the care of the ranch animals and, with Sam's assistance, she rode T.J. a handful of times in the arena.

The stocky cowboy glued himself to her side, babysitting her every move those first days, but inch by inch, day by day, he gave her space.

Yet, it was strange. From the minute she swung up into the saddle, her body took over, knowing instinctively what to do. With each passing jolt of the horse's stride, she became more confident in her job. She may not have been able to remember riding, but her limbs moved in rhythm with the horse at every turn.

Nighttime consisted of another matter altogether— lying awake, waiting for Nick's call. When he didn't phone, she'd toss and turn with disappointment over not hearing his voice. When he did, she'd dream of him.

Gradually though, his calls increased to every night. He claimed to check on her progress, to see if she enjoyed working on the ranch, while she asked about his trip.

"Do you miss the ranch when you're gone?" Pouring herself a glass of red wine, she went to the living room window.

"More than you know."

"When will you be back?" Staring out into the darkness she envisioned his truck pulling in.

"Late tomorrow night, but only for a couple of days. I figured it might help my sanity to check in."

"You mean to check on me?" Once or twice now, he let comments slip about her catastrophes on the ranch.

"Everything, Darc."

She shut her eyes and embraced the warmth flowing through her with the sound of her name on his lips.

"I tried calling my brothers—any idea why they aren't answering their phones this time?"

"They drove over to the Lonesome Steer for a couple of beers. "

"Why didn't you go?"

"Someone needed to stay here. Besides, a quiet night sounded better." *And I didn't want to miss your call.*

"Oh. I, ah, bought you something today."

Her pulse accelerated and wine sloshed over her hand. She set her goblet down on the end table and wiped her skin on her shorts. "What? Why?"

"It's nothin' big. I saw it and thought of you. No

big deal."

The fact he purchased anything for her loomed a huge deal. Uncomfortable with all the questions it stirred, she searched for another, safer subject.

"Have you talked to your parents?" She sat on her sofa, knees pulled to her chest.

"I spoke to my mom this morning. She's impressed with everything Sam's told her about you; wanted to call and talk to you herself, but Dad has kept her busy."

"How's he doing?"

"Good, but I hate that I can hear worry in my mother's voice."

Picking up the glass of wine, she sipped the liquid. "What's troubling her?"

"My father has an appointment Monday. Until she gets a good report from the doctor, she's pacing a hole in the floor."

"She loves him a lot, huh?"

"More than anything. I think buildin' the ranch from the ground up strengthened their bond." A deep sigh filled her ear. "If his appointment goes well, she's taking him on a cruise. One she hasn't informed him of yet."

"Sounds fun." Darcy reclined on the couch and closed her eyes, letting the low rumble of his gentle tones wash over her.

"I don't know. I'm not sure he's ready for the high seas. The last time I spoke with him, he wanted to come back and make sure we didn't bulldoze the place."

She snorted. "Like that would happen. He has to know how much you love the ranch."

"He does, but we weren't the most obedient boys growing up."

"I don't imagine any child is. How many years separate you and your brothers?"

"Eleven. I'm thirty-two, Sam's thirty, Trent's twenty-five, and Chris is twenty-one."

"At least you're close with your brothers." Again she wondered if she had a brother? A sister? She searched her brain, focusing hard to pull the information from the depths within her.

"Yeah."

She envisioned him sitting next to her, talking to her as an old acquaintance. Except a friend's voice didn't cause a tingly-tangly feeling to flow through every nerve ending in her body.

"Darc, what's wrong? You're distant tonight, darlin'." His endearments were becoming a regular part of his vocabulary.

Shivers traveled down her spine every time his southern voice spoke one. Before he left, she barely knew him. Now, on the phone, he edged close to being...more. Would the changes in the relationship hold true when he came home? Did she want it too?

"I, uh, was just thinking how lucky you all are to have each other."

Stop thinking of Nick in any other sense than a boss. You're only setting yourself up for heartbreak. Without knowing her past, any relationship remained out of the question, let alone one with her employer. She'd lose her heart *and* her job; the two went hand in hand.

"How come you don't talk about your family?"

She swallowed the ball of nerves forming in her chest, threatening to choke her.

"Things not good on the home front?" His tone

softened. "Come on, talk to me." The friendship with the eldest Matthews developed and matured over the last two weeks, but if she informed him of her amnesia, would he understand?

In the beginning maybe, but not now.

"Do you ever talk to your folks?"

"They ah...passed away." And somehow that rang true.

"Do you have brothers or sisters?"

The notion of lying to him any more hurt now that he had broken through her shell. She couldn't just blurt out, "I don't know. I can't remember." Her mind scurried for a way to distract him from the subject.

"Oh, geeze. Hold on. I spilled my wine." She made a rustling noise, taking the reprieve to calm her nerves. After a few breaths she returned with a quick, "Okay, I'm back."

"Drinking, Darc?"

"One glass. It helps me sleep after a busy week." Her hand rose to cover the yawn the words provoked.

"Don't get defensive on me. You're entitled to a drink. I'd like one myself right about now."

She swirled the remaining red liquid around in her glass. A comfortable silence stretched, and she closed her eyes, listening to his breathing. The sound soothed her, making her body languid along with the alcohol.

He sighed. "It's getting late. I should let you go. Hold down the fort until I get back."

Not wanting to let him go, she squeezed the phone.

"Darc, you fall asleep on me?"

An image of her head on his chest sprang to her mind. "No. But I should go. Night, Nick." Darcy hung up the phone, set her glass in the sink, and went to bed.

Her body hummed with the warmth of his tone while her mind grew troubled over the lies she told.

With conflicting emotions absorbing her every thought, sleep did not come easy despite the alcohol.

****

Nick tugged on his jeans, threw a T-shirt over his head and placed his feet in his boots, glad to be home. The phone calls to Darcy held him in suspense. His feelings for her remained a mystery to him. When he first left, he chalked up his attraction as just that—an attraction. She was a beautiful female; he a normal, hot-blooded male.

The mistake he made was checking in on her. The sound of her soft voice echoed in his mind. Without the stress of day-to-day life on the ranch, he found he longed to hear the sound of her laugh and her low, sultry voice before he fell asleep.

He went to the kitchen and poured himself a cup of coffee, thankful he remembered to set the programmable maker when he got in late last night. On his drive to the ranch, he called and rescheduled his last advertising meeting.

You're going through a lot of trouble for a woman, buddy.

Not any woman, Darcy. Though the fact remained she still held back when he brought up her family and her past, she warmed up to him during their conversations.

Downing the rest of his caffeine, he placed his mug in the sink, and went out the door. He squinted in the morning sunlight and started toward the equine barn. "Come on, boy," he called to Dakota, slapping the side of his thigh.

The boxy-headed dog ambled over.

Nick reached down to scratch him behind the ears. He glanced to the full water dish and half-eaten food.

"I see someone fed you." *About five feet two inches of heaven, no doubt*. From what Sam told him, Darcy had taken a liking to the dog.

He ambled across the way and grained the horses before letting the four-legged creatures out to pasture. T.J. kicked the wall in the last stall.

"Itching to run, fella?" Grabbing a hold of the gelding, he led the animal to his friends. By the time he finished filling water buckets and mucking stalls, sweat clung to his shirt. The weatherman promised the nineties by early afternoon. He peeled the wet material away from his body and used the cotton to wipe the water from his forehead. Tossing the shirt into the tack room, he moved on to the pig barn.

The petting zoo continued to be a success with the kids who stayed at the ranch, not to mention the few minutes of sanity for the parents. Another highlight if he bought a handful of placid horses for smaller, inexperienced riders—a possibility brought up during his trip.

Entering the pig pen, he sighed with relief. One of the guys beat him there. Or Darcy, another one of her regular pit stops in the morning according to Sam.

"Well, boy," he said to Dakota, who lounged outside the entrance. "Let's go see if the cabins are up to snuff for the next set of guests."

The sun penetrated Nick's skin as he sauntered over the three acres to the first cabin. He should've grabbed another shirt. After coming close to getting sun poisoning last year, he usually remained more cautious of the dangerous rays, but too many thoughts swirled in his mind this morning, too much eagerness to see one specific person.

Each of the twenty cabins sported the same undersized living room, a small kitchenette, a bathroom, and a bedroom or two. He approached the steps to the small porch of the cabin, opened the door, and advanced inside. The floors shone in the sunlight as cleaning fumes assaulted his nostrils. He shut the door and jogged his way to the adjacent building. Country music blared from the bungalow. Racing up the steps, he stopped in the open doorway.

Darcy swung her hips from one side to the other while sweeping—or dancing—with the broom. The impact of seeing her in the flesh caused his hands to grow wet with perspiration. After their nightly conversations, his attraction went more than skin deep, and acknowledging that fact scared the daylights out of him.

Give it up. She's an employee. And she deserved better than having her boss lust after her. He held no right to think of her in any other sense. The sexual attraction violated his ethics.

Even so, Nick bit his tongue to keep from chuckling out loud as she sang along off-key and moved through the room without a care in the world.

He stepped back to give her privacy only to trip on Dakota. The dog howled and in one sweeping movement, Darcy spun around, crossed the floor, and hit the power button on the radio.

"Nick!" She wiped the sweat from her face. "How long have you been standing there?"

"Not long." He cleared his throat and picked up a

rag off the floor.

Her cheeks heated to a nice shade of pink beneath her tan as she twisted the broom handle.

"Thanks for feeding Dakota."

"Your truck wasn't there when I went to bed. I figured you must have got in pretty late."

"Actually, it was early this morning."

"Then you should have slept in."

Her eyes darted to his chest, reminding him of his absent shirt. Her caressing gaze boosted his male pride to levels beyond. His skin tingled with every inch her brown orbs touched as her sights traveled up to his face.

"The place looks great. How 'bout we go on down to the main house and grab breakfast."

"I—I suppose I'm not going to get a better invitation. Unless we run into Horace, anyway." She started out the door. "You know he's my true love."

Her full, kissable lips turned up in a smile, a true genuine smile, one his brothers had privilege to, but not him.

Until now.

Nick followed her, taking note of the way she joked with him. He liked this playful attitude much better than the tension from before he left.

"Great, now I'm second to a pig. If he tries to steal away the first female companion I've had in weeks, he may find himself on a platter with an apple in his mouth."

Her eyes darted over him again, then widened with his words. "You wouldn't. Besides, I'm sure you've had plenty of dates."

The idea of entertaining didn't hold much appeal. Though, the way Darcy looked at him made him realize what he'd been missing.

"Where's your shirt? Didn't you learn anything last year?"

"How'd you know about that?"

"Chris told me how worried he'd been about you." She shrugged and kicked a pebble. "He filled me in on different things about each one of you."

"Did he now?"

This was news to Nick.

The past year, Chris acted as if he didn't care a scrap about his oldest brother.

"Mmm-hmm. Hey, wait for us, will ya? You have four legs, we have two," Darcy called out as Dakota ran ahead.

Beside him, she skidded to a stop, her head whipping from one direction to another.

Her skin paled beneath her tan. The expression marring her face resembled the day he'd hosed her off by the barn.

He searched the area noting nothing out of the ordinary. What made her so jumpy?

Her hand squeezed his bicep. "You ever feel like someone's watching you?" she whispered.

Chapter Six

"Come again?"

"You know, the hair on your neck standing up type sensations." Her wide eyes stared at the tree line.

On alert, he followed her gaze, curious over her odd behavior. "I don't see anyone."

"Sorry. Must be my overactive imagination again." She shrugged, but lingered for a moment, examining the area.

"You need food."

He steered her toward the house and trudged up the steps of the wooden porch, holding the door open for her, but uneasiness gnawed at his gut at her sudden mood change.

"Let me grab a shirt out of the dryer, and we'll get some breakfast." He crossed to the laundry room off the kitchen and pulled on a dark gray T-shirt.

"Where's Ms. Liz?" Darcy looked around the large kitchen and leaned on the center island.

"I'm sure she's around." He opened one of the large refrigerators, removed the bacon, sausage, fried potatoes, flapjacks, and scrambled eggs. At the last minute, he grabbed a jar of strawberry jelly.

The cook gave him an ear full on how *his* new employee put the stuff on everything she ate.

"If you come in after a meal, she always keeps

extra in the fridge." He set out to warm up the food and pointed to the island. "Can you grab the silverware? Center drawer."

"Sure." She carried the utensils into the spacious dining room.

Nick followed behind her and placed the food on the buffet table located in the center of the room. Smaller booths sat in front of the floor-to-ceiling windows. "Why in here?"

"I like the atmosphere. The fireplace is beautiful." Darcy scooped a spoonful of eggs on her plate, three strips of bacon, and a pancake.

Her calm demeanor a total contradiction from her paranoia moments ago. His narrowed glance followed her movements.

Not sure what to make of her, he viewed the ceiling to floor, stone-encased hearth and was reminded of the many fall months they'd spent cutting, splitting, and stacking wood with their father. One day in particular haunted him to this day. His father had carried an armload of wood into the house and told Nick to keep an eye on his brothers. Minutes later, they rushed Sam to the hospital for slicing his palm open on a chainsaw.

"Your family's lucky to have such a great place. I love working here. Your brothers have been very patient teaching me everything I need to know." She shifted in her seat, her leg brushing his.

His groin instantly tightened.

Don't go there. Relationships do not mix with business. To distract himself, he shoveled a forkful of eggs into his mouth while she dug into her own food.

"Are you excited about going on the camping trip?" he eventually asked.

"Yes." She broke off a piece of bacon and popped it into her mouth.

"It's an experience you won't forget."

"What happens on these overnighters?" Darcy spread strawberry jelly on her pancake. One by one, she placed the digits in her mouth and sucked the sticky mess off her fingers.

He imagined her tongue swirling around each one. The blood ran rapid through his veins, his heart pounded in his ears.

"You, ah—" He cleared his throat. "You ever go camping?"

She coughed, choking on her food.

Nick reached over and pounded her on the back. "You okay, darlin'?"

"Mmm-hmm." She took small sips of her coffee and stared at her plate. "No. I've never gone camping."

"Really? Wow." To everyone he knew, the recreation was part of growing up. How else did you learn about the great outdoors? Sure, a few of the women he dated didn't care for the activity, but they went at one point or another. He wanted a woman who appreciated the ranch and *all* the land had to offer.

Trent remained the only Matthews who came close to walking down the aisle. The bullet the surgeons cut out of his shoulder after an argument with his ex-fiancée soured the whole family's view on matrimony. Nick beat himself up for months after the incident for not protecting his brother—for failing to see how demented his future sister-in-law had been. Now the woman across from him brought coffee to her lips with a trembling hand, eyes darting in every direction but his. Uneasiness settled back in his gut.

"Well, I guess you're in for your first. We ride the horses to a spot not too far and bed down for a couple nights."

She straightened and smiled. "I think the riding will be my favorite part."

"Don't count out the rest of the experience." He chuckled, masking the concern churning inside. She didn't know how to muck stalls or what to feed the animals, but looked forward to handling the horses? The large creatures intimidated most people, but Darcy's face lit up with the prospect of being near them. She was more of a puzzle every day.

Her hand came up to smooth a strand of hair from her face. Once again, her gaze strayed from him. She ruffled the strands at her forehead covering the pale puckering skin at her hairline. This wasn't the first time the sparse, tiny, white marks on her hands called his attention. The notion of pressing her for details swirled on the tip of his tongue.

"Hey, Darcy, I didn't know you were in here. A guy called for you." Chris entered the dining room, plate piled with food.

"Yeah, right. I've had guys lining up at the door." She rolled her eyes upward and laughed.

"I'm serious." The youngest pulled out a chair at the end of the table.

Nick's gut clenched. "What did he want?"

"He asked if Darcy Brooks lived here. I told him you were out at the moment and he asked it again, 'Darcy Brooks is working and living there?'" He shoved a forkful of food into his mouth, continuing around the food. "I said, 'yes.' Then I asked his name or if he wanted to leave a message, but he hung up."

A look of alarm crossed her face. "Odd, don't you think?" She swiveled toward the windows.

"He could have seen you out, asked around, and someone pointed him in this direction."

"Yeah." She picked up her plate and headed toward the kitchen.

"Shouldn't you be headed for Tulsa, Nick?"

Catching a glimpse of the anguish on her face, he pushed his chair back. "I postponed."

A strange feeling swirled in the pit of his stomach. First, she thought someone watched her and now this.

"You keep putting it off, they're gonna refuse to meet with you."

"Yeah. I'll get there," he replied absently.

The idea of a man being interested in Darcy bothered him. She'd never mentioned another man. Was he a boyfriend from the past or a current one she'd failed to mention? If so, why was she so uneasy about the call? Could the guy be the reason she was so jumpy?

"If anyone calls again, get their name before you give out any more information," he told his brother. *At least until I figure out if there is any danger here.*

He hurried out the door after her. "Darcy?" Quickening his steps to catch her, he grabbed her arm as she continued sprinting away from him.

Darcy shook as she made her way across the yard. *So what if someone called? Big deal.* Months ago, she'd have jumped for joy at the notion—before she fell in love with her job, before she made a life for herself, before Ni—

"Stop." A large hand closed around her arm and pulled her to an even more impressive chest.

She swallowed the cry in the back of her throat and stared at Nick's torso. Her gaze traveled up to his concerned face.

"What's going on?" His eyes roamed over her.

"N-nothing. I'm fine." Wiggling her arm until he let go, she blinked to chase away any trace of emotion.

His hands fell to his sides; his eyes narrowed. "You weren't upset in there?" He jerked his thumb in the direction of the house.

"I'm fine. I'm sorry if I led you to believe otherwise." She bit her bottom lip to keep it from quivering. Realizing they stopped in the exact spot she felt someone watching her before, she rubbed her arms, waiting for the eerie sensation to envelop her, but it never came.

Between the renewed sensations of someone watching her and now a man calling, she didn't know what to think or where to turn.

Hold me, Nick, please. I need to feel the contact. Need to feel like I'm not alone in this world before the shadows swallow me.

"And here I thought we were working toward a friendship." Beefy arms folded over his chest and closed off any more images of him wrapping her in his embrace.

"Honestly, I'm fine." Her mind raced to the easiest explanation. "I was hoping to go into town and spend time with my friend Jordan." The idea of seeing her raised her spirits the instance she spoke the hasty-made plans.

His sights bore through her as if he read her every thought.

"I have to go. I'm okay, really." She spun on her

heels and fled to the barn before he saw too deep within her soul.

Her jangled nerves spiraled out of control. If she didn't get a handle on herself, he was sure to get suspicious.

Ha. Who am I kidding? He knew she hid something. Keeping her amnesia a secret from the Matthews family had sounded like a good idea in the beginning, but now she questioned her logic. Now she felt prisoner to her own mind.

She did need to see Jordan, someone who knew her secret.

****

"I can't believe you still haven't told him?" Jordan sat on the floral print sofa with her legs crossed. "I kept your secret from Tammy only because the information should come from you. I even understand why you didn't tell them during the interview with the other places denying you employment, but this has gone on long enough."

"I love my job. I don't want to lose it."

"You have to tell Nick." The nurse brushed her long blonde hair off her shoulder. Worry filled her blue eyes. "Keeping the amnesia to yourself is eating you alive. I can see the strain on your face."

"I can't." *It would be the end to my new world. The only one I know.*

"He called me, you know, to check up on your references." Eyebrows raised in her direction. "You told him you lived in Girard?"

"It was the first place to pop in my head." She cleaned the dirt out of one fingernail with another. What else had the two talked about? Was that what brought on the change in his attitude on the phone. "When did you talk with him?"

"About a week or two ago."

The same time the nightly talks started. "You didn't tell him about..."

"No. I promised you I wouldn't. Though, the idea did cross my mind. Especially when he threw questions at me regarding your life in Girard. I was able to deflect most of them by telling him I didn't know much about your life then."

"Thank you."

"I think you're making a horrific mistake, but I can't force you to tell him."

"I will eventually, in my own time." She flopped back on the couch. If she told him now, she'd destroy her newfound friendship.

Tired at the circle the conversation kept going in she said, "Enough about me. How's everything with Ed?" Darcy worried over the relationship. On their last conversation, Jordan informed her that the ex had come back in the picture, claiming he'd been a fool to leave her behind. Jordan seemed happy, but...

"He's good." She glanced down, fidgeting with her tan slacks.

Glancing around the room, Darcy only now noticed bare spots on the walls where decorative pictures once hung. She jumped to her feet in alarm.

"Jordan, what's going on? Where are your pictures?"

"I was going to call and have you come over, but work's been crazy, and then you beat me to it." She ran a finger along the seam of her pants. "I'm moving to Nashville with Ed." Conflicting emotions shown in her bright blue eyes.

Seeing the excitement her only family member tried but failed to mask, Darcy gnawed on her lip. "I thought you decided against the move. Isn't that why you broke up the last time?"

"I did. It was." Jordan grasped her hand. "But I love him, and he loves me, that's why he came back. He needs my support now more than ever."

While she admitted Ed sported a good voice and might make a go of being a country singer, she couldn't help resent him for taking her best friend—her only close friend—away.

"What about work?"

"I already have three interviews lined up at medical offices in Nashville. I'm sure I can land a good job. Dr. Sheffield has a friend there, he's going to speak to him personally." She took a deep breath. "I know this is sudden, but it feels right. I swear I'll call you."

"Make sure you do."

Tears filled her eyes as she hugged Jordan good-bye an hour later. The one person she considered family was deserting her. While she was happy for her friend, Darcy's own lonely, fake life reared its ugly head. No one knew the real her, the scared, amnesiac girl hiding deep within.

A shimmer of doubt filtered through. What if she injured herself, or someone else? What if she never remembered her old life? Then again, what if she did and the memories ruined her future on the ranch?

A fist squeezed tight in her stomach as she drove back to the ranch.

Walking up the steps to her home, she opened the door, kicked off her boots, and went to shower. The long day wore on her aching muscles. The hot water cascaded over her skin, but didn't release the tension in her shoulders. The knowledge of having Jordan move away, the one person who knew the truth, left her feeling more alone than when she'd woken up in the hospital.

As she towel dried her hair and ran fingers through the tangled strands, a knock sounded on the front door. She quickly threw on jeans and a tank top.

"Hold on." She dropped her towels in the hamper and hurried out to find Chris standing on her porch.

"Hey, we're all going to the Lonesome Steer for drinks. You wanna come with us?"

She pushed the screen door open for him to enter.

"Come on. It'll be fun."

Not wanting to be alone, she welcomed the invitation.

Chapter Seven

Trent parked his truck next to the wood-paneled honky tonk topped with a steer riding away from the large neon star.

After exiting, Nick moved the passenger seat forward to let Darcy and Chris out of the back. Her flowery scent filled his nostrils as she stepped down and walked with him through the entrance. He struggled with the need to approach her about the early afternoon events while another side of him longed to feel her body in his arms.

Needing air not consumed by her, he approached the bar along the back wall. "Hey, Gus, how's business?"

The tall, broad man turned. "Nick Matthews? What drags you out this way?" The owner fingered his handlebar moustache. "I heard you've been out of town more than in since your parents took up traveling. How they doin'?" He tugged on the ends of his black leather vest.

"Good."

A crash of balls along with a cowboy's hoot sounded from the pool tables tucked in the back corner.

The barkeep glanced at all of them. "Aren't you missing one? Where's Sam?"

Chris spoke up. "He stayed behind, but we brought

Darcy."

Nick's hand slid to the small of her back, ushering her forward. "Darc, this is Gus Rankin. He owns the place."

"Nice to meet you." She smiled and stuck her hand out.

"Pleasure, ma'am." A grin spread across his tanned face. "What can I get y'all?"

"Four beers?" Nick glanced to the group. Everyone nodded.

Long neck bottles were soon placed on the wooden bar.

"We have a new waitress, Pam," Gus told them. "She'll be around to see if y'all need refills or want to order food."

"You have a cook tonight, Gus?" Chris asked with a grin.

"We have a cook most nights, boy." He chuckled deep and rich. "Just hardly ever the same one."

A fiery redhead bumped into Chris from behind.

The woman balanced a tray on one slender hip and rubbed a hand over Chris's back. "Sorry, you okay, sweetie?"

Nick shook his head at his brother's goofy grin. Eyes wide the young stud nodded.

Gus removed the tray from her hands. "Pam, this is the Matthews clan. They own the dude ranch out on Hope Road."

"You want anything, just give me a holler." She winked at the runt.

"Let's get a table." Trent led the way through the room.

Nick ushered Darcy across the dance floor and

headed to one of the round tables. Unwilling to put much space between them, he pulled out a seat for her and seized the one on her right. Chris straddled a chair on the far end. Trent grabbed the remaining one.

"Let's do a toast to the last family who stayed in cabin three. Thank the good Lord they left. The kid was a brat," Trent stated with a snarl.

While his brothers recapped stories of past guests, Nick noted the strained smile on Darcy's face. She raised her beer and downed a good portion of the contents.

He nudged her leg. "You havin' a good time?"

"Sure." She drained the rest of her beer and motioned to Pam for another as the waitress drifted past the table.

Nick worried over her slamming down the barley. With her slight frame, the alcohol wouldn't take long to affect her.

"So, you two together or what? Romantically, I mean?" Pam placed a bottle in front of her.

"Never a good idea to mix business and pleasure," he answered automatically, raising his voice over the noise. A glance in Darcy's direction had him taken back by the hurt that flashed across her face.

He frowned. The comment wasn't meant against her personally, he simply stated the fact. Getting involved with an employee was wrong. Not to mention there were more questions surrounding her than answers.

"Anyone need anything?" The waitress asked, her breasts near spilling out of her low-cut shirt as she leaned over the table.

Nick noticed Darcy adjusted her own white, ribbed

tank top. The material clung to curves just large enough to fill his palms. His gaze traveled up her neck to her flushed cheeks.

"I'm good, thanks," he stated, keeping his attention on Darcy.

"I'll take one, and bring over four of those tequila shots." He heard Chris state.

"None for me. I'm driving," Trent mumbled.

"You know, it might do you good to relax once in awhile."

"If I did, you'd have to find another ride home, squirt."

"If you want to drink, I'll drive," Nick offered. "One is my limit, and I don't think these two are going to be ready to go for awhile." He flipped his thumbs toward Darcy and Chris.

Trent simply shook his head and leaned back in his chair.

"How 'bout you, Darcy?"

Her gaze slid up from peeling the label off her bottle. "Sure. Why not."

Nick stretched his arm along the back of her chair, absent-mindedly fingering a piece of her hair. Every now and again, as if drawn to her like a magnet of its own accord, his hand grazed her bare shoulder, igniting the sparks.

"Here you go." Pam returned seconds later, shots in hand.

"To another successful month at the ranch." Chris raised his glass.

Darcy raised the alcohol to her lips, grimacing as she swallowed. For the next half hour, the brothers shared more stories. She smiled from time to time, even gave a forced laugh, but when she glanced to him, he noted the bleakness of her gaze.

She shifted in her seat, her hip bumping him.

"I'm going to go mingle with the females in the joint," Christ announced.

"Yeah, and I see a couple of buddies over by the pool table. You two don't mind, do you?" Without waiting for a response, Trent headed off in one direction while Chris went in the other.

"How 'bout you?" Sweet lips turned his way.

"Nah. I'm too tired to entertain anyone. You?"

"Nope." She bent one leg up on the other. The music slowed and a couple of people filed onto the dance floor.

He noted her slumped shoulders, the forced upturn of her lips. Brown eyes lifted to his and her hair brushed his skin. Fingering the strands, he moved closer, needing to assuage whatever made her so sad tonight.

Dancing was the perfect excuse to embrace her without raising suspicion. He stood and extended his hand toward her. "Wanna dance?"

She stared at his open palm before tentatively placing hers in his. Nick's adrenaline built at the prospect of holding her in his arms.

Two more couples swirled around the hardwood as they reached the dance floor. He spun Darcy in a circle and drew her into a slow country dance, his arm going to the back of her neck as he positioned her at his side. She kept her head down, he assumed watching their feet.

Nick bent toward her ear. "Follow my lead. Right, left, back, forward, twirl."

As her body caught the rhythm, the DJ changed songs. His hands went to her slender hips, hers to his shoulders. Warmth spread through his chest as her fingers gripped his muscles.

She was close, but not near enough. With a hand on the small of her back, he urged her tighter to him. The feel of her played havoc on his spiraling hormones, and he wanted nothing more than to whisk her away where they could be alone. Remembering where they were, he let the music guide his actions and stepped forward, one foot between her legs then back.

She repeated his moves, her hips rotating against him in time with the beat.

His earlier attraction escalated with the intimacy of the dance. He questioned the logic in continuing the close contact. Furthering any relationship with her was out of the question, so why was he torturing himself this way?

Because it's a sweet pain. One he had a hard time denying himself.

Thigh to thigh, center to center, he struggled to keep his hormones under control.

Darcy closed the centimeters of space between them and brushed a fingertip across his torso. He frowned down into her intoxicating eyes. A body bumped into her, throwing her hard into his chest. All movement around them ceased as his gaze focused on the beauty in his arms.

Nick pulled her closer, caressing her slender hips. Wanting to feel so much more of her, his fingers wondered over her back, down her sides stopping on her rounded bottom.

The hot desire in her eyes rocked him, and his body

squeezed out any space leftover between them. When she rotated against him, the strain proved too much—he needed to back off before he lost control.

She ducked her head, and he let her conceal her face in his shirt while he attempted to quell the raging hormones threatening to burn him from the inside out. With his heart beating erratically in his chest, his thoughts jumbled in his head as the invasion of her flowery scent attacked his senses.

Lifting her head from his chest, she met his hot gaze with one of her own. Every cell in his body was on full alert. Her head fell back, exposing her long neck. He tangled his hand in her hair and guided her face back to him. His stomach muscles tightened as the need for her exceeded anything he'd ever encountered before. Hot lips branded his jaw as she bit at his chin.

Nick brought his hands up to feel the smoothness of her neck while running the pad of his thumb across her full bottom lip. Did she feel the heat? Share his sexual frustration? It was all too much. Hell, he *had* to taste her sweet, sinful mouth.

Before either held the ability to stop, lips touched, bodies meshed. The kiss was smooth, and not enough. A whirlpool of hunger, hot and raw, spiraled out of control. Explosions went off in his head, and he crushed her to him.

She whimpered in his mouth as fingers delved in his hair knocking his hat to the floor.

When his tongue tangled with hers in a dual, his brain short-circuited. She tasted better than he imagined, and a tremor went through his hands as he bracketed her face and nipped at her for more.

Her tongue flicked his lip, causing his senses to

skyrocket.

To hell with it.

He growled low in his throat and reclaimed her for his, slipping a hand to the back of her neck under her hair. A moan sounded in his ear. Seconds turned into minutes as he ravished her. When he slowed the kiss, nibbling her delectable flesh and gazed down at her, his body shook with need.

Then reality slowly invaded. They were in the middle of a dance floor at a bar for all to see. This wasn't right.

She stared at him with wide eyes.

"I'm sorry. I shouldn't have kissed you." He searched her face for any sign of—hell he didn't know—maybe for anything that might tell him what was going through her mind.

Darcy licked her lips. "I-I'm not." The words came out slurred.

In the heat of the moment he'd forgotten her drunken state. She certainly didn't kiss like she was three sheets to the wind. He shook his head and glanced around.

"I don't think anyone noticed. I can't even claim to be drunk. At least not from alcohol."

"I don't th-hink you can get drunk from secondhand fumes," she huffed.

Nick picked up his hat and placed it on his head. "That's not quite what I meant, darlin'." Grasping her hand, he led her off the dance floor.

The silent woman he devoured only seconds ago plunked down in the chair. As he lowered his throbbing body next to her, she scooted further away.

He frowned. "What's your problem? It's not as if I

forced myself on you. You were equally turned on."

"And now I'm sure you're embarrassed to be with me."

"What are you talking about?"

"Don't want to get caught messing around with the hired help."

Astounded over her outburst, Nick yanked her chair to his then froze. He wasn't embarrassed at being with her, but he was upset at losing control. Damn it he knew better than to get involved with an employee. Saying any of this to her would be adding fuel to her fire.

"Just rest until my brothers show up." He guided her head to his shoulder.

At first she refused but after minutes of fighting to stay upright, she rested it on him.

"Hey, bro, how's it going?" Chris smirked as he sauntered over to the table.

Nick ignored the gleam in his brother's eye. "You guys ready to go?"

"It's not even eleven o'clock, and I met up with a few friends."

"Quit whining. You're twenty-one, not twelve." *When will the boy grow up?*

"Who put a burr under your saddle?"

"I want to get Darcy home." Her breath caressed his arm as he studied the top of her head resting on his shoulder, causing his chest to tighten and making him feel drunk.

Drunk on a craving.

He needed to get away and regain control. Her kiss affected him more than he cared to admit. This growing attraction did neither of them a bit of good. A relationship complicated things.

"I think everyone's aware of that." A scowl marked his face. "What happened to our rule of not sleeping with the employees?"

"Boy, are you drunk, or just stupid?" Trent came up behind the runt and flicked him in the head. To Nick he added, "Hell of a show."

"Look, I know what happened out there can't happen." He gritted his teeth in embarrassment over his brothers seeing his lack of control. "Let's go. I need to get her home." He glanced to Darcy just as dark eyelashes lay on her creamy tan cheeks. Her head slipped toward the table. "I think she overdid it tonight."

Positioning his forearm in front, he slid the other behind and angled her to rest in the crook of his arm. The back of his finger ran over the soft skin, and a jolt of electricity ran through him. The one woman off-limits was the one who stole the breath from his lungs.

A throat cleared with a cough, and Nick glanced up to see concern on Trent's face.

"Right, let's go." Standing, he lifted Darcy into his arms.

"You take her home. I'm staying." Defiance shown in his youngest brother's features.

"Take the truck," Trent offered, handing over the keys. "I'll stay and make sure junior here gets home. We can catch a ride."

"You sure?"

"Yeah."

Trent helped him get Darcy settled in the truck then stepped back toward the old honky tonk. "You know what you're doing?"

Nick let out a heavy breath and rubbed the back of his neck. "I don't have a damn clue." And that was the truth.

"Good to know." His brother smiled, smacked the metal, and sauntered away.

"Hey, don't forget you and Chris are up for the morning feedings and chores. Darcy and I'll tend to the horses."

"Yeah, yeah." A hand waved the air as he disappeared into the building.

All the way home, he fought hard not to look at the dark-haired beauty sleeping next to him, because he wanted nothing more than to pull over and hold her. She remained the one woman he'd found who held his attention *and* loved his ranch. Yet, the idea of risking his heart spooked him. Not to mention her nervous moments, and the fact she might be keeping something from them. Being the oldest he bore the responsibility to protect his family despite his own feelings. Attraction or not, he wouldn't let another female wreak havoc on his family. No way was he willing to risk his brothers' lives for the sake of love.

Love. Ha.

He refused to believe his feelings possessed that level of intensity, not for a woman who kept part of herself hidden.

As he passed under a street light, he glanced at his passenger. Her brows creased. What was she dreaming about that was so disturbing? Vowing to find the underlying cause of her secrets, he turned up the drive to her cabin and got out.

Dakota barked and ambled over, tail wagging.

"Hey, boy, keep it down." Reaching out, he gave

him a scratch behind the ears. "Let's get the house open and put the little lady to bed." The lock clicked in the silence, and lights flicked on with a hit of the switch.

Retrieving his charge, he headed for her bedroom, laid her down on the comforter, pulled off her boots, and eyed the situation.

No way.

His restraint was not that strong; she'd have to sleep in her clothes.

He dropped to the edge of the bed and ran a thumb over her bottom lip. "You pack one hell of a kiss, darlin'," he whispered.

She sighed in her deep slumber and warm breath caressed his finger.

Damn.

He rubbed the back of his neck as he stood and shut the door on temptation.

Chapter Eight

Darcy rolled and pulled the pillow over her head to block the light coming from the window. The dull ache in her skull escalated to a hammering. She peaked at the clock beside her bed. *Eight o'clock.*

Nick expected her at the barn *two hours* ago.

Throwing the covers back, she jumped out of bed. A wave of dizziness washed over her forcing her to grab the edge of the dresser. A few deep breaths through the nose and out the mouth calmed her reeling senses. How had she gotten home? Last thing she recalled was dancing with Nick.

Oh, God.

Had Nick brought her back and put her to bed? She looked down. Thank goodness her clothes were still on.

Seeking headache medicine from the kitchen cupboard, she downed two pills and grabbed a bottle of water out of the fridge.

Nerves gnawed at her insides as she brushed her teeth, pulled on her boots, and hurried out the door. Alcohol might not have been her friend last night, but even the barley failed to mask the memories of Nick's kiss. Not much of the conversation had sunk in, yet the feeling of his lips on hers had been burned into her mind.

Only, the hot, tingling, and wanton thoughts were

new and exciting. She couldn't even remember what song they danced to, but the feel of vibrations pulsing through her veins remained strong.

Fighting to keep her eyes open in the bright sun, she retrieved her glasses from the car. The shades dulled the blinding light, but not the pounding in her head as she picked her way to the barns. Upon entering she found the object of her fantasies bent over a hoof in T.J.'s stall.

Nick's eyes caressed her as she opened the door and advanced closer. The army-green T-shirt stretched as he finished the job.

"Nice of you to join the living." Straightening, he leaned on the animals side.

"Sorry. I overslept." She licked her dry lips and focused on the dirt at her feet. His black boots stepped closer, and she forced herself to stand still.

As the heat and tension increased, her mind played back the scene at the Lonesome Steer. The dance. The kiss. Fluttering anticipation filled her. God, she wanted him to touch her.

"About last night..."

Pretend you don't know what he's talking about. The thunderous beat of her heart sounded in her ear. *No. Talk to him. Tell him...*

Darcy glanced up and cleared her throat. "You mean the kiss?" *The scorching hot entanglement of our lips.*

He stepped forward and removed the sunglasses.

"Yes." Lifting his hat, he ran a hand through his hair. "I've been up all night tryin' to figure this out. The only explanation I came up with was the alcohol."

A desire to punch him flooded her. Why couldn't

he admit he wanted her. Maybe he wasn't interested in a relationship? Maybe he'd only been caught up in the moment.

No. She refused to accept that. This game of pretending wore on her jangled nerves. Her belly tightened as she stared, even as her body warmed under his gaze.

"If...if the beer is the reason, why do I want to kiss you again?" she braved.

Seconds ticked and his brown gaze never wavered from her face. The sound of birds chirping outside the barn mixed with the pounding of her heart were the only noises she heard. She lowered her gaze to the toe of her boot. Had she gone too far?

A calloused finger raised her chin to his warm, searching gaze.

"How did we get to this point?"

She licked her lips and watched his Adam's apple move.

"It's not a good idea." His whisper held no merit as his warm mouth covered hers.

Darcy opened to him as his tongue slid into her delving round and round. Her knees weakened, threatening to give out. If not for the tight band of his arm around her, she'd be lying in a heap on the stall mats. How was this a bad idea when the feel of his expert mouth ravaging hers felt so right?

He invaded every inch of her mouth as his big body pushed her up against the wall.

The taste of coffee and toothpaste, heat and desire swirled. A moan escaped. She couldn't get enough as hands roved over her shoulders, down her back to her bottom, and squeezed the flesh.

A growl, the raw sound of his need escalated her internal temperature. Darcy whimpered and hooked her foot around the back of his leg.

"Nick, you in here?"

Her heart spiked with the sound of Trent's voice echoing through the barn as Nick tore his mouth from hers. Her body trembled with his sudden abandonment, and she wrapped her arms around her middle.

Running a hand down his face, Nick stared at her, but answered, "Yeah, what's up?" to his brother before stepping outside of the stall.

Boots clunked closer. "Have you seen Darcy? The runt is worried because she hasn't made her way over to the pigs yet."

"Chris is supposed to take care of the hogs today."

"I know, but she usually shows up anyway."

Darcy's heart thudded in her chest as Trent's watchful eyes traveled past his brother's shoulder into the stall, a questioning gaze flying from her face to Nick's.

"I told you last night, she's helping me with the horses."

"I'll...ah, let him know." The sound of Trent's boots clumped as he exited.

Muscles bunched under the cotton of Nick's shirt as he hung his head. "This can't happen." He turned away presenting her with his back. "Business and pleasure don't mix."

"I've heard." She bristled. Thanks to Chris, she knew all about the kind of women Mr. Authority dated in the past. "Which do I remind you of, the ones who wanted nothing to do with the ranch, or the one who pulled the gun on your brother?" Her blood reached the boiling point more from frustration than anger. It hurt to have him reject her. Hurt more because she was already so alone. And now she'd screwed up the one thing she did have—a job she loved—by throwing herself at him this morning.

"I know you're not like them, Darc." He shook his head, clipped a line under T.J.'s chin, and started to lead him out of the stall. "Let's talk later. Right now we have a horse to work with."

"Fine by me." She grabbed the rope out of his hand and whirled away. "I can do it."

"Darc?"

"*What?*" She spun back around.

"I know you aren't like the other women," his tone quiet, almost apologetic, "but my brothers and I agreed long before you came here not to mix relationships with the ranch."

"You mean you don't plan to let your girlfriends or wives share in the biggest part of your life?" Did he know how ridiculous he sounded?

Nick pinched the bridge of his nose. "Can we start today over?"

"I thought the day began fine. It's the last few minutes that need redone, but sure, you're the *boss*." The words flew from her mouth before she had a chance to stop them. Her insides twisted at the humiliation of falling all over him only to have him reject her.

His Stetson lowered, and he sighed. "Let's take him out to the corral today. Tomorrow we'll go on the trails."

For the remainder of the morning, Darcy sat in the saddle while Nick lunged the horse in a circle, making sure she knew how to stop, turn, and balance her weight in the saddle while T.J. cantered.

"You know this is pointless. I rode him while you were away." Every time she mounted up, her body took over where her mind refused to go.

"You rode him in the corral. We're taking him out on the trails. I have to be sure you know what you're doing, although you do ride like a natural." He continued driving him one way then the other.

Unable to help herself she stared at Nick, noting the shadow growth of the scruff he didn't shave and remembered the scrape of those bristles on her skin. The memory brought her hand to her cheek. Her mind raced to visions of him holding her in his arms, his lips on hers. Heat spread through her body, and she shifted her weight in the saddle.

The horse stopped.

"Why'd you stop him?"

"I didn't mean to."

"He's overly sensitive. Squeeze with your legs and cluck once."

She did, and T.J. began to walk.

"Now turn him yourself." Nick unhooked the line. "Go to the right."

Pushing with her left leg, she loosened one rein and tightened the other.

"Now to your left."

She directed the horse easily, moving as if they were one. The only thing rattling her nerves were the male eyes watching. Her mind jumped to another man helping her in the saddle, leading a horse down the road.

The sun shone high in the sky. A trickle of sweat

traveled down her back.

"Once you get comfortable with him, we won't need the rope."

"I think we're at that point now. Don't you, Captain?" She patted the side of the horse's neck.

Perspiration beaded on her brow. Her head pounded in her ears. Why was she having these flashes now?

The sun's rays intensified and over the next half hour she found it difficult to concentrate. Her mind held the images just out of reach.

Nick put the animal and her through more paces then called a stop.

"I think you've had enough. You seem tired. Maybe you should head in early."

"I'm fine."

Darcy dismounted, grabbed the rope, and hurried away to tend to the animal. Why was she getting glimpses of her past and not her full memory? A soothing feeling settled over her whenever she recalled the flashes; maybe that explained her comfort with the horses.

Finishing up, she released T.J. into the pasture and headed off to the cabins. In a hurry to get to Jordan's yesterday, she had left the last three for today.

What was she going to do about her attraction to Nick? He made clear his refusal to allow anything to develop, forcing her to face the cold, hard facts.

Getting down to business, she used the physical work to drown out the frustration until the bathrooms shone, the floors gleamed, her fingers were raw from the force she used.

The day's heat plastered her shirt to her skin and

her jeans to her legs. Standing, she wiped a forearm over her face. Sweat dripped down between her breasts as she dumped the dirty water out of the pail, put the cleaning supplies in the closet, and headed home for a much needed shower.

Cool water cascaded down her body dropping her internal temperature a few degrees until she shut the shower faucet off and stepped out of the tub.

After going through her nighttime procedure of applying cream to her scars, she pulled on gray cotton shorts and tank top, ran fingers through her tangled hair, then made her way to the kitchen to poured herself a glass of wine. A breeze blew through the open windows and screen door. She welcomed the cool air in the stuffy room.

A scuffling of boots on her porch caused a momentary startle. She spun around and gasped at the sight of all she desired standing on her porch.

Nick held a tan Stetson out toward her. "I forgot to give this to you."

She pushed the screen open and stepped aside for him to enter.

He placed the hat on her wet head and brushed strands of hair off her shoulder. "Looks good."

"Thank you, but you didn't have to get me anything." She'd forgotten he mentioned buying her a present.

"If not, your nose may permanently be burned." Thick shoulders shrugged.

He thought about my nose? Her belly filled with nerves. She handled this side of him much better over the phone. Maybe if she asked nice he'd go to his cabin and call her instead.

She touched the peeling skin then the brim of the sou'wester. Surprised he even bothered after this morning, she felt obligated to thank him in some way even if she was still embarrassed. "I...ah was having a glass of wine. Would you like one? Or I have water or beer," she said hastily as she hurried to the refrigerator.

"Beer would be great." He moved to the living room.

Gulping her wine in hopes of settling her nervous stomach, she topped off the glass, grabbed a bottle of beer, and returned to the living room.

"Here you go." Fingers brushed as she handed him the alcohol, causing a tingle to travel up her arm. "Thank you for the hat." She sat in the corner of the couch.

"You thanked me already."

"Right."

Darcy fretted with her fingers before glancing over at him on the opposite side of the couch. He stared at the label on his beer.

"Nick, what's up? I would think this to be the last place you'd want to be after this afternoon." She folded her feet under herself. "If this is about the kiss again—"

"No." He exhaled and laid his head back on the couch. "I wanted a place to hide out for a few minutes—guess I thought the hat seemed a good excuse."

"Hide from what?" Darcy frowned. Worry over what was going on made her gnaw at the inside of her cheek.

"My life." His eyes shut, and a muscle clenched in his jaw. "How'd everything get so messed up?"

She placed a tentative hand on his arm. "Want to

talk about it?"

Stress-filled eyes opened. "I received a certified letter from the attorney of a family who stayed here last month. They're suing the ranch."

"For what?" Hearing the alarm in her own voice, she cleared her throat and set the wine on the end table.

"A twelve-year-old broke his arm. He fell off the roof of the cabin, which we told him *multiple* times to stay off. We even spoke to his parents about the problem." He plucked off his hat and rubbed the back of his neck. "The mother claims the incident happened due to our negligence."

"Don't the guests have to sign a waiver relinquishing the ranch from liability?" Wanting to comfort him, to help him deal with his stress, Darcy moved a hesitant hand up to his shoulder and squeezed. Resistance met her fingers. Talk about tense. She dug deeper into his stiff muscles, which were tighter than the cords on a violin.

"Yes, but Mrs. Miller claims we falsely advertised activities to keep children busy." He groaned as her hand pressed harder. "We never claimed to be a damn babysitting service. We're here to entertain and educate, but when the kid refuses to participate, we can't drag them kicking and screaming."

The Matthews family worked hard at making the ranch a success. How dare the Millers try to ruin their reputation. "What did your mom say?"

"I haven't told her. She doesn't need the anxiety." He drained his beer, then stood.

Nodding to the bottle he set on the wooden end table, she asked, "You want another one?"

"No, thanks."

The tic in his jaw and tight line of his lips worried her.

Not knowing how to help ease his distress, she scooted back in her seat and picked up her glass. "What about your brothers? What did they say?"

"You're the only one who knows at the moment." Nick sat on the edge of the couch and placed his head in his hands. "I'm sorry. This really isn't your problem."

The defeat in his voice wore on her heart. He chose to talk to her above his brothers, sought comfort from her presence. Not giving in to her second, third, or even fourth thought, she set her wine down again and scuttled across the soft cushion, wedging herself behind him to massage the thick, tight muscles.

"You can't take this on yourself."

"I have to watch out for everyone and keep this place running."

He groaned as she dug her fingers into him. One by one, the tense cords loosened a fraction.

She stroked the couple of sexy, gray strands at his temple. "Your brothers are in this, too. Keep this up and you're bound to be completely gray by the time you're thirty-five."

"I'm the oldest. It's my job."

"Have you contacted the ranch's attorney? You should have legal representation."

"Yeah." He pulled away and rolled his neck, cracking the bones.

Feeling dismissed, she moved back to her seat.

"I'm waiting for Mr. White to call me back. He's the one who drew up the original waivers the guests sign."

"Don't speak to the Millers until you've spoken to

him." She sipped her wine. "You know the case has to go through the National Advertising Review Counsel and the Children's Advertising Review Unit before a decision can be made, right?"

Whoa. Where had that come from?

The glass wavered in her fingers, forcing her to hold it with both hands.

A frown formed on his lips. "How do you know?"

How did she? "Must have seen it on TV or something." Which was impossible considering she rarely watched television. She searched for anything else that could help him, but found no more.

Without a word, she picked up his bottle and went to retrieve another. What else hid in her past? The little bits of her memory surfacing lately were maddening, like a puzzle still missing the main pieces. Returning with the beer, she handed it to him.

"Thanks." He smirked, twisted off the lid, and drank.

She traced a finger along the rim of her glass and stared into her goblet. What was she to make of him coming here, bearing gifts, and seeking comfort? *Did* he want her as much as she wanted him?

"Darc, I'm sorry. I didn't mean to unload on you. It's nothing for you to worry about."

"I wish you'd share the burden with your family. This is their problem, too." His brothers looked up to him. The love flowing around the ranch left her wondering if anyone had ever loved her. Especially now that the one person she was closest with would be moving away.

She swirled the red liquid, noting it was half empty...Just like her life.

What was Jordan doing right now? The brush of warm fingers on her cheek as Nick tucked a strand of hair behind her ear brought her gaze up.

"Hey, why the frown?"

"Nothing..." She stared at him for a long moment. The compassion in his eyes made her eventually confess, "It's my friend, Jordan."

"The one you lived with before you came here?"

"She's moving to Nashville. Can you believe it?" She gulped her drink then continued. "Jordan and Ed don't have a great track record of staying together, and yet she's moving out of town with him."

"I'm sure you'll hear from her." He guzzled his alcohol.

She finished off her wine. "Yeah. I just hope she knows what she's doing."

"How come Jordan's the only person you talk about?"

His lowered voice caused a shiver to travel down her spine, and she swallowed the sigh in her throat.

The side of his lips lifted. "What?"

"Nothing."

Sitting here, talking with him as a friend, her emotions overflowed. A tear slipped down her cheek. A friend's voice didn't cause you to want to rip your clothes off and his. Her vision blurred as her rims filled with liquid. She only wished he was a good enough friend she could tell him everything—why Jordan's leaving made her feel so alone, about her accident and memory loss, and how thankful she was to be here on the ranch.

"Awe, hell, Darc, I didn't mean to make you upset. Come here."

"I don't know if that's such a good idea."

"Just come here," he said softly and tugged her over.

His soapy, male scent assaulted her nostrils as the warmth of his body seeped through her shirt.

He took the hat from her head and placed it together with his beer on the end table, then wrapped her deeper into his arms.

His spicy scent turned her brain to mush as she hid her face in his chest, absorbing his strength. The gentleness in the hand smoothing her hair back from her face created an ache deep within.

She rested her hand on his torso feeling the beat of his heart pounding under her palm, causing her breathing to quicken.

With a finger under her chin, he raised her face. His gaze probed hers.

She bit her lip. *Jump in. Live every minute to the fullest. Make new memories, a new life. Make him admit he feels it, too.*

"I should go." The words came out in a rush, but his hands held her in place.

Her eyes searched his handsome face. "Don't you want to stay?" *Please.*

"Damn." Nick's head lowered. His lips grazed her lips and pulled at the bottom rim before his mouth crushed hers.

She tasted beer, the alcohol proving more of a turn on than not. Not that she needed one. He was lethal by himself.

He lifted her leg, maneuvering her over him so she straddled his lap.

"We shouldn't do this." He breathed against her

cheek, licking his way to the sensitive spot behind her ear.

Oh, God. Waves of tiny sparks lit her skin.

Desperate to feel him, she slipped her hands beneath his shirt to caress his hot skin, letting her fingers memorize the dips and plains of every muscle, scraping a nail lightly across his raised nipple. His teeth nipped her throat, and moisture dampened her shorts as she rotated her hips on the coarseness of his jeans.

"If you keep that up, I'm gonna explode."

The pressure of his hands on her hips held her in place. His heavy breath caressed her hair as he raised his head and stared.

Did he feel as crazy as she did? Her fingers traveled his upper body, past his thick collarbone and through his hair. Heat like an inferno absorbed her as she tugged his mouth back to hers.

His finger traced the V of her tank and drew the material down. "God, you're sexy."

The ache within her built. She thrust her breasts toward him, wanting, searching for more.

This isn't a good idea, he's my boss.

His thumb grazed her pebbled nipples, and all thoughts of the right thing to do vanished into thin air. As she tasted the salty skin of his neck, she pressed her breasts to his chest.

He groaned, and his fingers dug into her inner thighs, brushing her most intimate part. How could this be so wrong when it felt so right?

Chapter Nine

Pushing her head up and noting the dazed expression, Nick questioned the logic in staying any longer.

Logic, hell.

He'd thrown any common sense out the window the minute he picked up her hat and stood on her porch. The image of her lying beneath him refused to leave his mind—the swell of her breast, her long legs, and flat stomach. His fingers flexed and unflexed with the idea of pulling her shirt up to reveal her skin. A need, raw and primitive, raced through his veins.

Slow down.

If this thing between them stood any chance, he needed to let the feelings mature. *Stood a chance?* When had he decided to move forward? The notion bothered and elated him.

Delicate hands came up to rest on either side of his cheeks and the beautiful gaze searched his features. He only wished he knew what she looked for.

Bringing her mouth down, she grazed his chin, and he groaned. As much as the idea of ending the make-out scene killed him, he placed a finger over her lips to slow her down.

She sucked his finger into her mouth; her tongue swirled around the digit.

It took every ounce of his being not to give in to the urge to lay her back and show her what she did to him. "Darc..."

Eyes glazed over with passion, her head went back, exposing her flesh.

His restraint slipped as his finger traveled down her chin to trace the smooth column of her throat. Testosterone guided his moves, making any coherent thought impossible to grasp. He brought her mouth to his and plunged inside, his tongue seeking, exploring, wanting more.

Delicate fingers bunched his shirt to the center of his torso, the cool air kissing his burning skin.

Nick propelled her to lie back on the couch and raised the hem of her tank top. Never had he been aware of every nerve ending in his body. Just one more minute of this torturous, glorifying hell before he called a halt.

Gazing down at her flushed cheeks and red, swollen lips, she made the picture-perfect image of hot sex.

With one hand he smoothed her hair back while his other caressed her breast, her hip, and moved down her thigh. He placed his lips on her navel and tugged the waistband of her shorts down a fraction. The salt of her exposed flesh lingered on his tongue.

He tugged her leg up and stopped short at the sight of a large scar on her inner thigh.

"What happened?"

She pushed him off and stood in one quick motion, straightening her cloths with jerky movements. "I...I was in a car accident a while ago."

"How long ago was your accident? It must have

been recent for the mark to still be there."

Picking up her empty glass and his bottle, she hurried to the kitchen. "It will always be there."

When he imagined what she must have gone through, concern filled him. He followed her to the sink and placed his arms on either side of her. Her head bowed forward.

"You get hurt anywhere else?" Not able to resist, his lips suckled the back of her neck.

"It's over, so let's just drop it, okay?"

Feeling somewhat out of balance at the new questions arising, he conceded to her request. "For now, if that's what you want, but know this"—he shifted her around and motioned a finger between them—"can't be a one-night fling. It'd make your job here too difficult." He ran a finger down her soft, silky skin. "We have to be sure we want to take this to the next stage—for both our sakes."

"Didn't we already?"

He rested his forehead on hers before kissing her brow. Anything more than the brief contact he was sure to take her on the damn floor.

"I should go. Don't forget we're riding in the morning."

****

Darcy pushed the hair back from her face and repositioned her new hat, images of the previous night never far from her mind. She'd tossed and turned during the night with a yearning Nick fueled and the torment his words brought.

"You ready?"

Leading a buckskinned horse, the object of her agony entered the barn. He crossed to T.J.'s stall and put an arm around her waist, pulling her to his chest. The smell of horse and leather, man and spice caused a whimper to escape as his lips brushed hers.

This is not the time or the place. Not that that stopped her from enjoying the feel of him.

"Mornin'." His eyes darkened. "You taste like heaven."

"And what does heaven taste like?" She rested one hand on his tanned forearm and stared up into his sexy face. The feelings he aroused were new and frightening. She didn't want to jeopardize her job or friendships, but to ignore the growing attraction between Nick and herself held the same effect of denying the air she needed to breathe.

"You." His smile lit up his eyes as he stepped away to put his horse's lead rope through a bracket on the wall.

Instantly, she missed the contact.

"This is Ben."

She stroked the side of the horse's neck. "Hi, Ben."

"Let's get T.J.'s bridle on and we can ride."

A smile touched her lips at the notion of getting back in the saddle—the one familiar place.

"Here." He handed her the bridle and stepped forward to inspect the saddle she'd already put on T.J.'s back.

As he tightened the cinch, she slipped the straps over the horse's head and buckled the end.

"Not bad. I'll help you mount, then I want to show you the trails we've made in the woods. Once the guests arrive, we'll be setting off on a two-night adventure."

A hand squeezed her knee, causing a spiral of

nerves to giddy up through her. The idea of sleeping with this cowboy under a blanket of stars warmed her cheeks.

Nick sauntered over to Ben, opened the gate, and led both horses through before mounting his own.

Darcy glanced at the woods up ahead. Peace and serenity, her mind cleared. She straightened her shoulders, her muscles loosening and moving in rhythm with the horse.

The muscles in his back moved when he shifted, and she recalled the warmth in those arms when they were wrapped around her, the safe, content feeling that had washed over her when he held her.

"Wanna trot?" A thick leg brushing hers found her next to the man in question.

His horse danced at the notion. "He knows I'm restless," Nick said with a wink.

She sucked in her bottom lip. "Definitely."

"Remember, if you wanna stop, sit back in the saddle and take a deep breath. If he doesn't respond, pull his head around to your knee with one rein." He demonstrated with his own mount.

"I'll be fine."

"Give him a slight squeeze with your legs and cluck once. If he doesn't move, tap him—"

"I got it already." She squeezed and clucked before he finished his instructions.

T.J. picked up the pace in an instant following the trail ahead of him.

Joy and excitement filled Darcy as her bottom rocked in the seat with each jolt. She urged him faster. Wind whipped through her hair. Her eyes watered. Laughter rang in her ears.

Laughter.

The spotted horse picked up speed, and she laughed harder as a red barn loomed in front of her.

"I told you, you could do it, baby girl." Warm arms hugged her as she hopped down from the saddle. A floral perfume surrounded her.

"You looked great up there, kiddo."

She laughed as an army uniform picked her up and twirled her around.

Angry eyes of a younger man glared in her direction as the older gentleman set her feet on the ground.

"Didn't she do good, Lance?"

"Yeah, sure. She's perfect," the boy snarled. "As always."

"Whoa!"

The loud voice startled Darcy. A hand filled her vision, reaching over to grab her reins. T.J. came to an abrupt stop, and she flew forward into the saddle horn, her chin bouncing off the horse's neck.

"Darcy?"

She blinked until Nick's concerned features came into view.

He dismounted and held on to her horse's reins. "What the hell were you doing?"

"What? I-I'm..." She took in her surroundings noting the absence of a red barn. A panicky feeling washed over her. Sweat beaded under her shirt. Where was the couple who embraced her?

Dark eyes glared. "I called to you, but you didn't answer."

"I'm sorry. I got lost in my thoughts."

A doubtful look crossed his features, teeth tightly

gritted together. "Get down. *Now.*"

Oh God. I screwed up. She swung her leg over the horse's rump and once her feet hit the ground found herself pulled into Nick's arms. "You veered off the path and came close to going face first into the ravine."

He pointed a few feet beyond the trees where the bank dropped off to a bottomless pit surrounded by ridged rocks.

She swallowed. Her heart hammered in her chest and bile rose in her throat. The memory was so vivid she would've sworn it was real.

"Why'd you go off the path?"

"I-I don't know." She rubbed her temples. More flashes of her past. The gentle man. The reddish-brown haired woman. The angry boy.

"Darc, what's going on?" He grasped her shoulders, his eyes penetrating hers.

Hands forced her shoulders down, holding her trapped as he tried to kiss her. She screamed and kicked as a door crashed open.

"Get off..."

Darcy yanked away from the hands. Not able to decipher her vision from the present, she lowered her head and stared at ground. How did she explain her glimpses of the past?

"Look at *me*, damn it."

Slowly she raised her head.

Concern and anger shown in Nick's features. The tight clench of his jaw and cold stare made her step back.

"This stops here and now. Something's been wrong since the day you came here. I can't help you if you don't tell me."

Jordan's words came back at her. *"You have to tell him. What if something happens?"*

"I want to know *now*."

"I had a flashback," she blurted out.

"A flashback?" Brown eyes narrowed. "Can you elaborate please?"

She snared several deep breaths before answering. "Remember the car accident I mentioned? Well, since the eighteen-wheeler smashed into my car, I haven't been able to remember anything of my past." She glanced at the ground then at his handsome face.

Disbelief and confusion registered in his eyes. Arms folded across his chest. "You have amnesia?"

"Yes."

A long moment passed as he studied her. The urge to squirm under his intense glare escalated.

"My God. You're serious."

"Yes."

"Does anyone on the ranch know?"

She kicked at a stone with the toe of her boot. "N-no."

"Did the idea ever occur to you to tell one of us? What if something serious happened? Hell, Darcy, you could have killed yourself just now." His arms flailed out in exasperation.

"I know." She rubbed her temples again. "I'm sorry."

"Do you remember anything? Your family?"

"I don't even know if I have one."

"What about Jordan? Does she know?"

"Yes. We became friends when she was my nurse. She let me stay with her until my memory came back...but it never did so..."

"You moved in with a stranger." His eyes widened then narrowed, and he shook his head. "You accepted this job without saying a word."

"Everyone's a stranger to me, Nick. And would you have hired me if you knew?"

The answer lay in his frown.

"No one else did either. I needed this job. I wanted a *life*." Frustrated tears ran down her face, but she refused to acknowledge the weakness. "Tell me how you'd feel—I had no family, no job, no friends, and no idea where I'm from. I don't even know what my favorite food is."

"Strawberry jelly."

"What?"

His lips gave a little quirk. "Your favorite food. You put strawberry jelly on everything; your toast, your pancakes, your crackers. I've even seen you put it on meatloaf.

He's right. How did he...

Her head pounded and knees threatened to give out. "Can we go back, please?"

Nick crossed to his horse, extracted a rope out of his saddlebag, clipped it onto her horse's bridle and secured the line to Ben. "Mount up."

Longing to curl up on her bed and sleep the rest of the day away, she pulled tight, heavy muscles into the saddle.

Nick slid a glance to the woman beside him. He didn't have a clue as to what went through Darcy's mind when she'd raced past him with the most beautiful, carefree smile plastered on her lips. At first, he believed her having fun—only to have his stomach lurch to his throat when she led her horse toward the ravine.

Now her face was pale and pinched and she sat ramrod straight.

"I'm sorry."

He strained to hear her words and surveyed the vacant look in her eyes. "Darc?"

A hand swiped at her nose as her sniffle caused an ache in his chest.

He sighed in anger and frustration warred with compassion and the need to comfort her. His concern for her safety scared him spitless. And now he questioned her sanity.

See what happens when I let my guard down. Was there other side effects to the brain injury and memory loss? Did she pose a threat to herself? To his family? Deep down, he believed her not capable of hurting a fly. But...

"We need to figure out what happens from here. The guests are scheduled to arrive tomorrow." He lifted his hat and ran a hand through his sweaty hair. "I'm not comfortable letting you ride. I can't take the risk of you having another flashback and hurting one of the guests, or yourself."

She swiped at her cheek. "I'll pack my bags as soon as we get back to the barn."

The opening to the barn came into view and he stopped the equine, unhooked the line, and angled Ben in order for him to see her face. He reached over, lifted her chin, and scanned her haunted eyes.

Damn. How did she get under his skin in the span of weeks? Words refused to form on his tongue. He wanted to wrap her in his arms and soothe her until she grew strong again, but the ranch and the safety of everyone came before his own desires.

His thumb swiped away a tear from her cheek, and she pulled back.

Nick let his hand fall to his side, offering her a tight smile while his gaze bore into hers. "It's evident you love to ride. Your face lit up like I've never seen."

The woman next to him frowned and nodded as she reached down to pat T.J. on the side of his neck. When she straightened, he tugged on her reins and nudged his mount to a walk. Together, the horses strolled to the barn.

"Go back to the cabin and take a long bath," he instructed as he helped her dismount.

Nick watched her defeated form as she wondered off. One step forward, three steps back. When the guests arrived, her responsibilities would increase. He needed her capable of handling the added pressure. Her job required her to see to the guests' comfort, to be attentive, and to accompany him on the two-night retreat. He needed to be able to trust her...and he wasn't sure he could.

Where was his head? He couldn't keep her on at the ranch.

Yet, the idea of letting her go cut straight to his heart. Who'd help her through this?

With a shake of his head, he removed the tack from each horse, placed the bridles on the hook, lugged the saddles off the equines' backs, and released them into the pasture before heading to the main house.

The notion of encountering any of his brothers made him hurry to the den. Sam sat at the big mahogany desk, the ranch expense books open in front of him. Unfortunately, his brother looked up as he stepped back.

"Wait, just the person I wanted to talk to."

"What about?" Nick crossed the threshold and shut the door.

"You tell me first?" His muscle-bound brother closed the ledger and scowled. "You look like hell."

"It's Darcy." Nick sat, then stood, then paced the length of the beige room. "Do you have her physical form?"

Shuffling through the papers on the desk, Sam said, "Trent probably put it with her employee file." He crossed to the wooden cabinet and rummaged through the content. "Here you go."

Nick scanned the pages and hit the table. Nowhere did it say anything about amnesia.

The incident bugged him, and as hard as he tried to convince himself, not because she was an employee, but because he cared for her more with each passing day.

Did these flashes happen often? He needed to talk to her, to see her, and reassure himself she was okay. First, he wanted to talk with someone who could give him more information. He noticed the signature and number on the bottom of the page. "I need to get a hold of her doctor." *For everyone's safety...and my sanity.*

"What's this about?"

"I took her out on T.J. to show her the trails. We weren't halfway to the camping area when she shot past me. I called to her, but she kept going." He scrubbed a hand down his face. "God, Sam she came within five feet of going over the ravine before I stopped that horse."

"What? Is she okay? Where is she now?" He

started toward the door. "That damn animal seemed fine in the corral."

"She's okay...I think. I sent her back to the cabin. But it wasn't T.J. She totally zoned out, claimed she had a flashback or something, that she has amnesia from a car accident."

Taking advantage of his brother's stunned silence, he dialed the phone with shaking fingers.

"Who you callin'?"

"Her doctor."

"You're serious?"

"Yes." He slammed the receiver on the desk. "Answering machine, damn it. Apparently he's on vacation." Nick ran his hand threw his hair. "Guests are scheduled to arrive in a matter of hours. And now I find out there's something mentally wrong with Darcy." He sucked in oxygen. "I'm not sure if she's stable enough to keep employed here."

"Come on, you can't fire her." He shook his head with a grim set of his lips. "She's not a nutcase. So she's had some sort of head trauma." Big shoulders lifted. "In the month she's been here, this is the only incident I'm aware of. We'll get through this. We'll help her figure this out." The calm one stuck his hand out palm up.

His gaze strayed to Sam's hand. The scar from the chainsaw wrapped all the way around to his palm. He'd gotten lucky the blade stopped before the teeth cut it completely off, a feat the doctor claimed was thanks to Nick's quick thinking and fast action.

To this day, Nick remained clueless as to exactly what he had done to stop the chainsaw, but in his book, he hadn't intervened soon enough.

That accident never should have happened.

And Trent never should have been shot.

"I don't want to...but I can't take the chance on any more accidents."

"Like the one with the Millers?" Tanned skin with a jagged white line across the center swiped a letter from the desk. "Why didn't you tell me we're being sued?"

Chapter Ten

"Damn." Nick hit the cabinet and paced the floor. "It's nothing for you to worry over. I'm working on getting it straightened out."

"Yeah, I know. Mr. White called looking for you."

He directed every ounce of his attention on his brother. "What did he say?"

"Not to worry. The Millers have no supporting arguments. Turns out Mrs. Miller sued another ranch last year. White said he does have to wait for a review counsel or review unit or some crap."

"The National Advertising Review Counsel and the Children's Review Unit?"

"Yeah, that's it." He nodded and reclaimed the seat behind the desk.

Darcy was right. Tension built along his neck. A cracking sound filled the air as he forced taut muscles one way then the other.

Was her memory returning?

"He wants to meet with you the day after tomorrow."

Nick shook his head. "I'll be out on the camping trip with the Lynwood group."

"I'll meet with him then."

"No. I should handle it. You go on the outing, but remember to keep Darcy close. This is her first time out and with the incident today—" Was he really considering letting her go?

"Nick—"

"No. I don't want any problems."

"Nick—"

"I'll tell her to sit this one out. There's plenty to keep her busy here. Chris can go in her place. Besides, I'm not sure what the right course of action is with her right now." He walked over to the window. She'd be upset, but she'd understand. The chance of her hurting herself, or someone else, was too great a risk.

"*Nick!*"

His head whipped around to frowning brown eyes. "What?"

"*I'm* going to handle White. Don't worry, we'll get things straightened out." He came out from behind the desk and sat on the edge in front of Nick. "But you should have told us. You need to realize you're not alone here. We're all in this together. Trent, Chris, you, *and* me."

Shaking his head in denial, a jackhammer started working on his temples.

"When are you going to quit taking everything on yourself? We aren't teenagers anymore. We're old enough to take on the pressures of the business." His self-appointed counselor scowled. "And stop staring at my hand. *I* moved the guard on the blade, not you."

His head snapped up to stare at his brother. "I was supposed to watch you."

"You were twelve at the time. Jesus, Nick, we all did stupid stuff." He grabbed an envelope off the desk. "Now let me deal with the attorneys. You go on the overnighter."

For him to relinquish his stress to his siblings went against every grain of his being. Taking care of them had hung on his shoulders for as long as he remembered. While his father and mother handled the growth of the ranch, it was his responsibility to keep the younger brothers in line.

"No."

"You can argue with me all you want. Your mind won't be on anything other than Darcy anyway." Sam leaned on his thighs looking to his brother with a raised brow. "You wanna tell me why that is? Don't get me wrong, I'm concerned about her too, but you're close to irrational at this point." He glanced out the window then back to Nick. "Heard about the kiss at the Lonesome Steer..."

Nick pinched the bridge of his nose. Tension rose at amazing speed, threatening to snap him like twig. He rubbed the back of his neck.

"You have strong feelings for her? I mean enough to jump in head first?"

He crossed to the window and stared unseeing out the glassy plains. His siblings had no idea how much he cared for her. Hell, he was having a hard time grasping the level in which his emotions rose himself.

"We'll help with her amnesia, take her to a doctor, whatever, but you have to stop taking everything on yourself. Christ, I'm thirty years old. It's about time you realize you aren't responsible for me anymore." Sam placed a hand on his shoulder and grinned. "I like Darcy. I'd like to see you two get together."

He nodded. "Me too." But with her doctor being on vacation, the only way he was going to get any answers was to ask her.

He excused himself from Sam's company and headed to her cabin. Two knocks produced no answer. Pushing his Stetson further back on his head, he rapped hard on the side of the screen door.

"Darcy?"

No response.

To hell with it. He pulled the barrier open and found her sitting on the couch with her knees drawn to her chest, a piece of paper dangling between her fingers.

She glanced up, and the pain in her features tore at his heart. Wanting nothing more than to take her in his arms, he held himself stiff in front of her. His emotions in turmoil.

"Want to talk about today?"

She lowered her forehead to her knees. "No."

He slowly lowered his frame to sit on the coffee table across from her. "I looked over your physical. It seems there's details missing."

"I know." She placed her bare feet on the floor and met his gaze. "Please try to understand. I spent over a week in the hospital. I had no recollection of my life. None. No one came to see me. No one called. Nothing."

Her tear-streaked cheeks were his undoing. His heart sank with the need to make sure she got through this. How was it possible to fall for a woman who didn't know who she was—and fall hard?

"I couldn't remember a thing." She rubbed a finger over the back of her hand.

"What does that mean? Did you have to relearn how to eat and dress? Did you know how to talk, walk?"

"No, I had my motor skills. What I didn't

know...what I *don't* know is what I did before now, who my family is, my friends, or why I moved here." She glanced at the paper she held in her fingers.

"What's that?"

Darcy handed the pages to him. "The missing details of my physical."

He examined the print, which clearly explained the extent of her injuries.

"I asked Dr. Sheffield to write everything on here. I planned to talk to your mom, but chickened out. I was afraid she'd fire me before I ever had the job."

Reading and rereading the report, words failed him. Between the written information and her words, while angry with her for holding back the truth, the reality of her situation hit him. The physical and emotional pain she experienced sank in. How alone she must have felt. Still felt.

He sat next to her and rubbed a hand over her back. "We'll figure it out."

"We?" Her half laugh filled the room.

"Yeah. In case you haven't noticed this thing between us"—he pointed back and forth— "isn't going away. If anything, it's gotten stronger. At least for me."

"Me too."

At her quiet admission, he closed his eyes. "God, Darc, do you realize how bad your accident could have been?" He let his fingers slide down her cheek to tuck her hair behind her ear.

She rose to her feet and crossed to the mirror on the wall, playing with her hair, angling the strands to cover the white line on her forehead. "Yes, just these ugly, puckered scars...and no memory. I'm lucky."

Rising, his body soon filled the space behind her.

His gaze met hers through the glass. Hurt and anguish shown bright in her eyes.

Nick kissed her cheek and rotated her to face him. "You're beautiful." He brushed the strands away from her hairline, placing his lips to the puckered flesh before pulling her into his arms. A hand skimmed its way up his torso igniting every inch only to settle over the pounding of his heart. His hold tightened as he brushed his jaw against soft skin.

Never had he experienced a need so strong. The need to protect her from whatever she may or may not find in her future flowed through his veins. He brought the white mark across her hand to his mouth. Inch by inch, he kissed his way over her digits, up her arm to her collarbone where he nipped her flesh.

She whimpered, and that's all it took. One little sound from her and he was a goner.

Nick groaned, pressing her to the wall. Her lips fastened on his while delicate hands roved over his body, igniting him with every touch. Adrenaline surged.

Seizing her wrists in his, he placed her hands over her head while working his way down to her cleavage. He bent his knees, bringing his sights level with her breasts. Nipples puckered under the thin fabric indicated her braless state. Dizzy with the knowledge, his lips closed over the peak. The cotton barrier dampened with his saliva, and she moaned.

Frustration of not being close enough made him release her arms so his fingers could work her T-shirt up.

"Let's go to the bedroom."

Her whispered words penetrated his ears as if she used a loud horn. He jerked back and regarded her for a second, then before either of them changed their mind, he picked her up in his arms, making the journey in three strides.

Once in her room, he laid her on the bed. The image of her lying with her lips slightly parted, her skin flushed with desire, was sure to haunt him every minute of his day and night.

He glided the back of his hand over her beautiful cheekbones to her jaw to the pulse beating in her neck. Fingers reached out and traced the five o'clock shadow covering his face. Taking every once of control, he held still while she brought her head up and licked the skin on his neck. A chill ran down his spine as she tasted him, bringing every nerve ending to full sensitivity. He held his breath while she pushed his shirt up and kissed his nipples. His testicles drew up tight.

Wanting to give her better access, he rose up on his knees and stripped off his shirt. She moved from one muscle to the next at an agonizingly slow pace, making her way down to his abdomen, navel, then lower. The tip of her fingers brushed his engorged state, forcing him to suck in a breath. Within a second she undid his pants, tracing the outline of him through his boxer briefs.

Not able to take much more, he propelled her to lie down.

"What's fair is fair."

Slowly, Nick drew her tank top up her torso and kissed each exposed section. In haste, he rid her of the garment and gazed down at her body. Perfection from head to toe. He licked the salt from her skin, his teeth scraping her creamy flesh.

"You're beautiful."

His finger traced the outside of her breasts, cupped the weight of them in his palm, and squeezed. Blood thumped through his veins to his groin. A craving greater than any he experienced spiraled deep in him. He ached, his body wanting more...now.

Her head went back into the pillow. Sweet hands touched his chest and pushed until he fell to his back. A knee angled over his body as she straddled him and traced a finger down his chest and around his nipples. His erection pulsated under her heat.

The sensations coursing through his body were exquisite and torturous at the same time. He pulled her head down to delve into her mouth. She kissed him back with vehemence while his fingers kneaded her breast, tweaking the protruding peak.

He tasted the delectable spice of her from her chest to the waistband of her jeans. The desire to explore and experience every gorgeous inch of her burning flesh prompted him to rip off her denim and panties in one fluid movement. He captured her beautiful, glowing body in his mind as he brought his closer to hers. His mouth closed over her dark nub, scraping the peak with his teeth, laving the skin with his tongue, then blowing on the sensitive area.

She hissed and grasped his biceps. "Nick..." His name came out thick and husky on her lips.

Nick set out to explore every inch of her, kissing her from head to toe, wanting to remember every sound she made, every intake of breath, every moan of pleasure passing her lips. His hand nudged her legs apart for his fingers to delve into her moist center. Her thighs parted further as he coaxed her body open.

Shivering under his attentions, she gasped and

panted. He withdrew and cupped the mound arching into his palm. Needing to take her higher, his lips trailed up her quivering muscles, stopping to place tender kisses on the puckered skin so close to where he desperately wanted to be.

Nick sat back on his heels, taking a moment to compose his raging hormones. Her tanned nakedness in contrast with white sheets struck him deep. Beautiful cheekbones flushed with passion, lips slightly parted, eyelids half closed with longing remained a picture he wasn't soon to forget. His gaze moved lower to the thin strip of hair covering the very center of her heaven. He spread her with his thumbs and inhaled her intoxicating scent before lowering.

Her hips bucked off the bed. She panted and ran her fingers through his hair, searing him to her.

Holding her with one hand on her belly, he suckled and drank in her sweet nectar, her cries of pleasure filling his ears as she climaxed. Hands roamed over him, grabbing at him, tugging him up her perspiring body. The realization he didn't have a condom hit him like a bucket of cold water, and he froze.

"What's wrong?" The confusion on her face caused an ache in his chest.

Resting his forehead on hers, he confessed, "No condom."

A devilish smile lit her face before she rolled over and opened the bedside table. "I found these in here when I was unpacking." She tossed him a sealed box of protection.

Not bothering to question where they came from, he ripped the package open and rolled one on.

Gazing down into her angelic face, he entered her

at an agonizing pace. Her eyes widened and lips parted as he sank fully into her, pausing to savor the feel of her surrounding him. Cupping his buttocks, she pulled him to her, gyrating her hips against him. Losing control, he drove into her, but refused himself release until she climbed back up to the top of the ecstasy ladder.

Teeth gnawed at her lips as her head pushed back exposing the column of her neck.

Running his tongue across the salty skin, he bit her earlobe then raised his head. "Look at me," Nick demanded.

Her gaze found his, and he watched her beautiful face flushed with passion. He drove himself into her as deeply as possible. Her body tightened, convulsing, squeezing him. The need for release urged him faster. He called her name as he reached his peak and collapsed on top of her.

Moments later, breathing slowed, Nick moved to lie by her side, using his arm to pillow her head. He pushed her damp hair back from her face and raised her hand to his lips.

No matter what her past, he wanted, *needed* to be part of this woman's future. With the silent admission, warmth filled his chest.

He kissed the top of her head. "I wish I had been there to hold you after your accident."

"You're here now," she whispered.

He pulled her closer and held her tight.

****

Darcy cuddled closer to Nick, listening to the beat of his heart as his warm skin branded her cheek. For months, no one held her, helped her face the world, her fears. Now, the man she suspected she'd fallen in love with kissed her and woke her body in the most sensual ways, emotions clogged her throat, and she sniffed.

"You cryin'?" Nick's deep voice asked in a whisper. The side of his thumb rubbed her cheek.

"No. I'm okay." Her lips brushed across his chest.

He moaned. "We'll never get out of this bed if you don't stop."

"That's a bad thing?" She flicked her tongue over his hardened nipple.

"I'd stay here for the rest of my life if it were possible." He raised her chin with his finger. "You blew through my life so fast it's taken me these past few days to realize what you mean to me." His lips grazed hers. "A relationship between us is going to complicate things, but I don't see any way around it. You've gotten in my heart, and I don't want to let you out." With a small chuckle, he shook his head. "I suck at this."

She placed her hands on either side of his face and kissed him. "You're wonderful." The feelings that started on day one now bubbled over, and she couldn't go on without exploring this thing between them, but she understood his concern. Their relationship deserved a chance.

What if you're already in a relationship—with someone else?

She shook the idea from her head. No memories of another man had surfaced, even now.

"Hey, where'd you go?"

The incredible man at her side nuzzled her neck and came around to her mouth. He shifted and pushed her head back to his chest while his hands roamed under the sheets to her thigh.

"I know you have a lot to work through. We'll take

it slow."

Fingers trickled over the top of the mound between her legs and her breathing quickened in anticipation, heat working up from her toes.

"I love watching your facial expressions when I touch you here."

A gasp escaped her lips and a tingling started low. His touch made her crazy with want.

The screen door creaked then banged on the frame instantaneously causing Darcy to feel a sense of loss as Nick withdrew from her.

"Darcy, you in here?" Chris stopped in the bedroom doorway. "Have you seen..." His gaze darted back and forth between the two, to her lover's bare chest, to the clothes on the floor...

Chapter Eleven

Darcy scurried up in the bed, pulling the sheets with her, not quite sure what to say to the youngest Matthews who glared then turned his back.

"Guess so."

"Chris, what the hell are you doing here?" Nick kicked the sheet off, and stood buck naked. "You can't just barge into someone's bedroom."

"The guests arrived early. I'll get them settled in the cabins and tell 'em to be ready to hit the trails in a couple of hours." His slender form advanced out of sight to the front door. "Sam drove the chuck wagon to the camp site," he hollered back, the screen slamming shut behind him.

"Damn." The distressed cowboy rubbed the back of his neck.

Darcy went up on her knees and kissed his bare shoulder, her belly brushing his naked backside. "Do you think he'll be okay? I don't want any of your brothers to hate me."

Nicked turned to face her and wrapped his arms around her waist. "They could never hate you. Trent and Sam will be okay. Chris is probably only in shock at finding us together. I'll talk with him." Resting his chin on her head, he continued. "How did he get in anyway?"

"I don't think we locked the door last night. Guess I had more important things on my mind."

A kiss touched her forehead. "We should head to the barn and meet with the guests."

Trailing her hand down his back to his buttocks, she squeezed.

"I guess they can wait a few more minutes for us," he growled.

"Us? You mean I can keep my job? I wasn't sure."

He held her away from him, his eyes narrowed as he studied her for a long moment. "Is that what this was about?"

She pulled out of his hold. The blunt words inflicted more hurt than if he'd slapped her. "How could you think such a thing?" She grabbed the T-shirt off the foot of the bed and pulled the cotton over her head. *Damn the stupid man*. Did he not see how much she cared for him?

"If you stopped and looked at it from my side you'd understand."

"What I understand is you aren't the man I thought you were." A horrible pang of hurt seized her. It was as if he plunged a knife into her heart while the shadows swallowed her lonely soul.

"Forget I said anything." A hand clasped her arm, drawing her into him.

Yanking her arm away, she sidestepped. "No. I can't believe you think I'd stoop so low. I'm going to take a shower then I'll come down to the barn. You can let me know the status of my employment when I get there."

"Darc..." His big, imposing form stepped toward her.

"No." She held up a hand. "I need time to myself, and I think you should figure out what you want. I know how I feel for you. I know I kept my amnesia from you, but if you believe I'd stoop to such levels to keep a job, you *don't* know me at all."

Tears pricked the corner of her eyes. Refusing to allow him to see how much he hurt her, she hurried to the shower and slammed the door. A second later, his boots clunked on the wooden floor, then the screen banged shut.

Stepping under the warm spray, she released the tears she held at bay and let the water wash her heartache away. This past month, she'd made things happen. She had taken control, left her past behind her, and embraced her new life. The best part was feeling her love for Nick grow every day. No, the greatest part was having his strong arms around her, feeling his love back.

What I thought was his love.

She sank to her knees in the porcelain tub. If he turned her away now, her life was over—again.

I've pulled myself up out of the dark before, I can do it again.

For the next two hours, she mulled over the past month, causing more and more heartache until she threw herself into cleaning up her cabin in order to keep occupied. She wiped off already clean counters, stripped the sheets from her bed, anything to prolong the time facing Nick. By the time she was sure other people would be at the barn, she almost had her emotions in check.

"Figured you'd be down sooner or later. The guests are getting acquainted with the horses and picking out their mounts." Chris stood at the entrance, cocking his head to the side, he touched her shoulder. "Hey, you okay?"

"Perfect." But her gaze drifted to where the eldest Matthews talked with a female guest.

A tender hand pressed to her back. "Want me to knock him out?"

Touched by Chris's concern, and thankful he wasn't mad at her, Darcy grinned. "I'll be okay."

"That's what I like to see." He pulled her close to his side. "You really fell for him, huh?"

She nodded and bit her lip. *Not here. Not now. No more tears, damn it.*

"You're sure you don't want me to punch him in the jaw?"

She shook her head and stepped away in time to see the one who stole her heart move in her direction.

No. Not now. Not yet. Her heart pounded in her chest. Refusing to engage in a confrontation with him in front of everyone, she started in the opposite direction, but stumbled when his voice sounded directly behind her.

"Okay, everyone."

His hand circled her arm, halting her escape and sending a jolt of heat up her arm.

"Time to get this show on the road. Lead your horse out of the barn. Once we check everyone's tack, we'll be off," Nick continued to the group. "I'm not real good with names, but I promise to try my best. In case anyone forgot, my name is Nick. That's Trent." He nodded to his brother in front of him. "He was your guide the last time y'all were here. Chris and Sam will be staying behind to tend the ranch while we're gone."

He pulled Darcy closer. "And this is Darcy."

He squeezed her shoulder, and she made a project of repositioning her hat.

"She'll be going with us."

Her gaze flew to his face, noting the grin on his lips as his eyes caressed her.

Nick hoped the lift of Darcy's lips indicated her forgiveness. He wanted nothing more than the day's activities to get underway so he could find a second to be alone with her.

Reluctantly letting her go in order to accomplish the task, he crossed to Sam as his brother finished checking one of the horses.

"I want to know every detail of the meeting," Nick informed him, keeping his voice low. "Text me."

"I know." Sam stepped back, shaking his head.

"Better yet, I should stay here. You go camping. Or send Chris." But then what about Darcy? Wishing he could take back his accusations of why she had made love with him, he glanced her way.

"No. For once, you're going to quit taking this ranch on yourself." A beefy hand landed on his shoulder. "You need to trust us, trust your gut, and trust your feelings for Darcy."

Nick backed up. His brother's newfound superior tone left little room for argument.

"Don't you think I blame myself for not seeing the trouble before it struck?" Sam continued. "You aren't the only one who feels guilty. Just thank God Dad has avoided any further heart problems, and I didn't lose my hand, and Trent wasn't killed."

"*You* felt guilty."

A hand rose. "Let me finish. April had a chemical

imbalance. She was severely bipolar and refused to take her medicine. Dad let stress get to him instead of talking and letting Mom or us help lessen the burden. Do you want to be like him? Hell, at this rate, you're going to end up having the heart attack Mom's trying to help Dad prevent."

All these years, he'd focused on how *he* failed everyone, not once considering anyone else shouldered the blame.

"Think about it. Besides, that woman needs you, and for some unknown reason wants you." A finger jabbed him in the chest. "And I hope to hell you know what you're doin' with her."

He gave a contorted chuckle and rubbed the back of his neck. "That makes two of us."

"Because if you screw this up, I'm gonna kick *your* ass."

Nick turned to face the reason for his heartache. A thrill ran through him at the prospect of holding her again. No other woman's kisses made his toes curl with want nor had he possessed the desire to stick to a female's side through thick and thin, the good and the bad. He'd help her through this. Be there for her at every turn. She was now the reason he breathed. She was his life.

"Everyone's ready," Trent confirmed, approaching with his horse.

Nick moved to his mount, adjusted the girth, and made sure his tack was in order. He glanced up to see that everyone was ready when he spotted Sam approaching the group by the barn, a dark-haired man close behind.

His brother's serious expression brought Chris and

Trent across the dirt.

What now?

Nick ambled over to Darcy and reached for her ice-cold hand as his brother neared.

"Something wrong?"

"Guys, this is Lance Brooks. He..." Sam shifted his weight. "He says he's Darcy's husband."

A cold wave of anguish swept over Nick as the words echoed through his being. Pressing his lips together, he glanced to Darcy, and released her fingers.

Her face turned ashen. "My...my husband?"

"Hi, baby. I've missed you." Lance pulled her into his arms. "Took me *forever* to find you."

Nausea rose in the pit of Nick's stomach.

"Thanks for taking care of her." The guy addressed him with a smug smirk before turning back to Darcy. "I'm glad you're okay." He tilted her head up and placed a full open mouth kiss on her lips, his eyes open, watching Nick.

Fist clenched, breathing became difficult over the raging boil of his blood. He spun on his heel before he released his frustrations on her husband's face.

Husband? Darcy's married? The earth shifted under his feet, and his stomach dropped. No, this wasn't right. He glance back to where Lance caressed Darcy's face. She didn't look like she was happy to see him.

Lance glared at Nick then drew back, both hands now in her hair, and went in for another kiss.

Bile rose in his throat, and he stepped toward them. No way was he going to stand there and let the man paw all over *his* woman.

"He's her husband, Nick." Trent grabbed his arm, his voice only loud enough for Nick to hear.

A sharp pain ripped through his chest at the apparent truth. He yanked his arm away, unable to stand around and watch the reunion.

"Come on, let's get this show on the road," he snapped. "The guests are getting antsy."

"W-what about me?" Darcy called, running to join them.

Nick glanced to his brothers and noted the sympathy in their faces before they lowered their heads.

A thin, cool hand touched him, and he turned. Confusion, hurt, and fear crossed Darcy's features. Unable to help himself, he wrapped her in his arms one last time and wished for everything to go away, for *Lance* to go away.

"You stay and get reacquainted with your hus...husband." Acid ate at his insides.

He kissed her forehead and placed her away from him. Forcing himself to walk away, he mounted his horse.

"Please, wait."

She started his way, but Lance grabbed her roughly by the arm. "Come on, sweetheart, let the cowboy do his ranch thing. We have lots of lost time to make up for." He pulled her to him, knocking her hat to the ground. "I can't wait to get you to the hotel."

Her distressed voice cried out, and Nick was off his horse in an instant. His blood pressure reached the boiling point. Husband or not, the man needed a few lessons on how to treat a woman. *Especially* Darcy.

"Let go." Darcy attempted to pull her arm away and stomped on the man's foot with the heel of her boot.

"We don't treat women like that around here,"

Nick growled from behind the slimeball holding his girl.

His brothers came up behind him.

"Nothing to concern yourself with. I'm sure once we have time alone, Darcy'll remember how it is between us." He snarled. "We have a long, *long* history. Don't we, baby?" His hand roamed down her backside.

"Get your hands off her, *now*." Never before did he think himself capable of choking the life out of someone with his bare hands.

"I don't think this is any of your business, *cowboy*." Lance released her abruptly and stepped toward him.

Darcy stumbled, but he saw Chris catch her arm and steady her.

"Darcy is on my ranch, and I won't have anyone manhandle her."

"No one but *you* right?" He laughed, then spit. "Oh yeah, I've been scoping the place out from the day she started here. I've seen you two together, dancing, riding." He glared at Nick. "Pawing at each other on her couch."

"You son of a—"

"You...you watched me."

The panic in Darcy's faint voice provoked Nick to move between her and this lunatic.

"You don't have to go with this guy, ya know," Chris told her, and put his arm around her shoulders. "You can stay here with us."

Lance stepped up to Nick. "Yes, she does. You think I'm going to leave her here for *him* to screw some more?" The husband pointed in Nick's face.

Darcy couldn't believe what was happening.

Instinctively, she went to Nick and touched his arm. He flinched, and she withdrew her hand. Did he think this man was telling the truth? All those times she imagined someone watching her, it was this man? Lance? Her *husband*?

Her skin crawled...and a bright light flashed.

A man and woman standing in front of the barn, hugging her as she approached.

"You're a natural. You were born to ride. Isn't that right, Lance?"

She turned and smiled at the boy. A younger version of the man standing before her.

Her vision swam. Darcy swayed as the standoff continued.

"I think this has gone on long enough." Sam moved between the two men. "I think it's time you leave. Trent, see to the guests. Chris and I will talk with Darcy and see what she wants to do. If she doesn't want to leave with you, she's not."

Nick didn't move, neither did his gaze waver from the man.

"I'm not leaving without her." Lance stepped in her direction.

Nick stepped to block Lance. "We'll just see about that."

A teenage boy held her down, trying to kiss her.

"Get off!" She screamed and kicked until the door of her bedroom crashed open.

"Lance, what are you doing? Get off of your sister."

Violent eyes squinted as the boy snarled.

Lance was her brother?

With a strangled cry, she wheeled away from the

group.

Her ears rang.

Her vision blurred.

She stumbled and covered her ears to block out the ringing.

"Darcy?" Chris's voice sounded far off in the distance.

She heard her name being called again, then Nick's as the sound mixed with the buzzing just as everything vanished into blackness.

Chapter Twelve

Darcy struggled to return from the darkened corner of her mind. The pounding in her skull discouraged her from opening her eyes. She moaned.

"I think she's waking up," a familiar male voice stated from above her.

"Darcy, Darcy?" Nick's deep voice came from a distance.

She blinked, fighting against the urge to close out the blinding light.

"Hey, sleepyhead, come on."

Her vision cleared slowly, from Chris, to the crowd gathering, to Trent, and to the warm body holding her. "Nick?"

"Right here, darlin'."

His tone rumbled in her head, which was pillowed against his chest.

"What..." She licked her dry lips.

"Here, sip this." Trent handed her a bottle of water.

With Nick's assistance, she grasped the plastic container in her shaking hand. The cool liquid made its way to her mouth, dousing her parched throat. "What happened?"

"You passed out," Chris answered and hunkered down beside her.

Her heart jumped as she looked up into faces of

people she didn't know. "Who are all these people?" She struggled to sit up, panicked.

Strong arms tightened around her. "The guests, remember? We were about to go camping."

Deep concern shown on Nick's handsome face, causing her to touch his stubbled cheek.

"I think that's my job, cowboy." Her so-called husband appeared above her.

"Come on, people, get back with your horses. Just a little setback," Sam called. "She's gonna be fine. We'll get this show on the road in a few minutes."

Mind reeling through the commotion, her head snapped up. Memories, voices, faces came rushing in. Lance wasn't her husband. She rubbed her temples as the hammering in her skull increased. Trying to understand it all, the fog cleared and pieces began to come together in her mind. Images of her mother marrying her stepfather, his son, Lance.

Lance was her stepbrother.

"We're not married," she informed them. "He's my stepbrother, *not* my husband."

Nick pulled back with an expression full of questions.

A lump of emotion rose in her throat. After all this time, she knew her past, where she came from. And it all paled in comparison to the anxiety she felt about her future with Nick. God, did she have a future with him? Did he feel as strong a connection to her as she did him? Uncertainty filled her, causing a tear to slip down her cheek. She shut her eyes and snuggled into his warmth, blocking out the doubts, savoring the safety of his embrace.

"I'm serious. I remember. I remember everything.

I'm not married to him or anyone else."

Her chin was raised and a hard kiss landed on her mouth. She smiled at Nick, her heart overflowing.

He lifted her to her feet, placed a strong arm about her waist, and rested his forehead on hers with a sexy little smile on his sinful lips.

She was free to love Nick, to be with him.

Lance approached from the side. "Get your hands off my wife."

"You sure you're okay," Nick asked her.

She nodded.

"Sam, hold onto her." When his brother stepped to her side, Nick released his hold. The fist he landed on Lance's face laid the disillusioned man flat out on the ground.

"Sam, do something." Although her stepbrother deserved it, she didn't want to see anyone hurt any further.

"Nick, stop," Sam shouted, but made no effort to intervene.

"I think you broke my nose. I'll sue you for this." Lance touched the sides of his injured part.

"Go ahead and do that." Nick opened his fist and shook out his fingers before flipping the other man over. He clasped Lance's wrist behind his back. "Chris, throw me a rope and someone call the police. Tell them we have a stalker and all-around dirtbag trespassing on the ranch."

After Nick secured the man's hands, her cowboy hauled Lance up by his wrists, causing a string of profanities to flow from his mouth. "Keep watch over Darcy's *stepbrother*."

Sam took a hold of Lance's arm. "With pleasure."

Not able to stay away any longer, Darcy wrapped her arms around Nick's waist.

"I called the sheriff's department," Trent said rejoining the crowd. "They're sending a car over."

"I'm taking Darcy to my cabin so she can rest. When the authorities get here, send the officers over there." He picked her up in his arms and crushed her to his rock-hard chest.

All these months she waited to remember her past, but none of it mattered right now. The only thing she cared about was her future. Her throat tightened and ached with suppressed emotions.

Nick entered his cabin and crossed to a room in the back of his home. Laying her down on a big bed, he stretched out beside her and propped his head in his hand. God, she was beautiful. He traced a knuckle down the side of her angelic face. He loved the way her smile began in her eyes. Happiness clogged his throat. Unable to stop himself, he kissed the tip of her nose.

Thank God, she wasn't married. He wasn't sure how he would have overcome the hurt of her leaving. Elation overflowed. The warmth of her breath caressed his face as his lips met her soft ones.

"Every time I kiss you, you take me to heaven," he whispered before slipping inside. He kissed her until his insides grew tight with want.

She groaned as he pulled away.

A calloused finger landed on her lips, rubbing over the rim. "I love you, Darcy Brooks. I think I have since the day you starting working here—part of the reason I stayed away in the beginning."

"That only prolonged the inevitable. Think of how much more time we would have had." She ran a hand down his chest.

He tenderly nipped at her flesh, regretting the need to finish the conversation before they could embark on the ride of their life.

"I know you have a life wherever you lived before now, but I can't go on without you." He took a shaky breath. "My life doesn't make any sense without you now."

She frowned and squinted, seeming to pull the info out of the newfound memories. "I gave up that life two weeks before the accident. I quit my job and moved here to hide from someone stalking me."

"Lance?"

"I'm pretty sure." She sat up, cross-legged on the bed. "I think he resented the attention his dad gave me, especially after my mom died. There were a couple instances where...he approached me thinking I wanted to fool around with him." She picked up their laced fingers and played with his digits. "One time he forced himself on me, but his dad walked in before he got too far. Then about a year ago, I received heavy-breathing phone calls, threatening letters. I thought the stalker could be a client of the law firm I worked for or a family member of one of the clients, but then Lance started showing up at the functions and restaurants I went to."

Nick pulled her closer to his body needing to feel her, to protect her, to keep himself from marching back to the barn to tear Lance limb from limb. "What about the cops?"

"They couldn't do anything; I had no proof."

"We have proof now. Everyone out there heard him say he watched us." Nick forced himself to remain calm while he encased her face with his hands, directing all his focus on her. "But I want to hear more about *you*. What did you do back home?"

"I worked as a paralegal in a law firm in New York."

"Big city girl, huh? That's how you knew about the review counsel." He rubbed a strand of her hair between his fingers. "How'd you end up in Amarillo?" Would she be happy living a country life?

"I was tired of looking over my shoulder and one night just left everything behind and drove, and drove." She shrugged. "There was something about this place that drew me in." Flipping over on her side, her hand rested on his chest. "I love it here. I...I love you. I want to be with you."

Gazing into her eyes, he got lost in a sea of emotions. "Stay here on the ranch, move in with me, be my wife." He held her between his hands afraid if he let go, she'd vanish from him. "Maybe you could even get a job at Mr. White's office. I mean, if you want to stay in that line of business. Or you can work here with me."

She jumped on her knees and landed on top of him. "Yes, yes, yes." She rained kisses all over his face stopping only when a knock sounded on the door.

"I should get that."

Reluctantly, he got up and went to open the door.

"Nick, this is Officer Callahan. He has questions for y'all," Sam informed him.

"I'll go get Darcy." Not going far from her side, he escorted his love to the living room and stayed glued to her while she recited everything she told Nick to the officer.

Officer Callahan jotted down notes and asked

endless questions. "My partner has Mr. Brooks in the car. We'll take him into town and press charges after I get statements from the guests."

"Thank you, officer." Darcy stood and followed him to the door.

As the cop left, Nick placed an arm around her waist.

Grateful for the support, she leaned into him, and he turned with her in his arms toward Sam.

"How are the guests? Anyone demanding a refund?"

"No. I told them as soon as the police were done, Trent and Chris would get them on their way." He smiled and rocked on his heels. "More good news— while I was waiting for the police, Mr. White called. It seems when he informed Mrs. Miller about contacting the previous ranch she sued, she dropped all the charges."

"Really?" Darcy said with delight.

"What did you say?" Disbelief registered on Nick's face.

"The ranch is free and clear."

How could this day get any better? With Lance behind bars, her memory being back, the ranch was cleared, and she was marrying the love of her life. Placing a palm on each of his cheeks, she pulled him to her and captured his lips.

A throat cleared. "I'll ah...let myself out."

Groaning, Nick's mouth left hers and a hand urged her head under his chin.

"Sam, wait. I want you to be the first to know...we're getting married."

"What?" A gleeful shriek sounded from the door.

"Hi, Mom." Nick hugged the woman with one arm, preventing Darcy from moving with the other.

"Mom? Dad? What are you doing here?" the second eldest asked as he kissed his mother's cheek.

"Samuel, Nicholas." Tammy Matthews kissed her sons, giving Darcy a wink and a smile. "Hello, Darcy." She stepped forward and embraced her. "Did I hear correctly? You two are getting married."

"Y-yes." Heat rose to her cheeks, as her fiancé stared down at her with a goofy grin on his.

"See, I was right." Tammy looked over her shoulder to her husband and pushed dark blond hair out of her face.

"It's not nice to gloat," Nick Sr. informed her with a smile.

"What are you talking about?" Nick frowned at his mother.

"You two. I suspected there was something between you two from the beginning. A few phone calls to your brothers confirmed it." With a permanent smile, she whispered, "Now, if I can just get the rest of my boys to settle down."

"Tam," his father warned in a low voice. "Leave the kids alone." He grasped her hand. "Let's go up to the main house and someone can tell me what the heck is going on out there. We drove up as police were driving away, and the guests are standing around laughing."

"I'll fill you in up at the house," Sam offered.

"We'll see you two later?" Nick Sr. spun his wife around before she could object and guided her outside.

"How long do you think we have before your ma shows up at the door again?" Darcy tucked her head on his shoulder, loving the solid strength of him as he lifted her into his arms.

"I'm counting on my brothers to keep her busy for a long time, because I plan on keeping you occupied all night." He kicked the door shut and locked the bolt.

The sound echoed, causing excitement to race through her. "You know, yesterday I didn't know who I was or where I was going."

"And now?" He followed her down on the bed and ran a large hand over her body awakening her senses.

"I don't feel lost anymore. I know exactly what I want." She hooked her arms around his neck, pulling his face down to her. "And I want you, Nick Matthews."

A word about the author...

Sherri Thomas enjoys being outdoors, spending time with her family, and tending to her many animals. If she's not in the barn, on an ATV, or horseback riding, you can find her reading or writing a romance novel—with the wonderful chaos of her four children and dogs in the background.

She loves to hear from her readers. You can reach her at:

sherrit4@yahoo.com

or drop a comment at

Sherrithomas.blogspot.com

Thank you for purchasing
this publication of The Wild Rose Press, Inc.
For other wonderful stories of romance,
please visit our on-line bookstore at
www.thewildrosepress.com.

For questions or more information
contact us at
info@thewildrosepress.com.

The Wild Rose Press, Inc.
www.thewildrosepress.com

To visit with authors of
The Wild Rose Press, Inc.
join our yahoo loop at
http://groups.yahoo.com/group/thewildrosepress/